The Lieutenant
of Kouta

The Lieutenant

of Kouta

Massa Makan Diabaté

TRANSLATED BY Shane Auerbach AND David Yost

MICHIGAN STATE UNIVERSITY PRESS | East Lansing

♾ The paper used in this publication meets the minimum requirements
of ANSI/NISO Z39.48-1992 (R 1997) (Permanence of Paper).

Michigan State University Press
East Lansing, Michigan 48823-5245

David Yost dedicates this translation to Lucy and Dale.

Printed and bound in the United States of America.

26 25 24 23 22 21 20 19 18 17   1 2 3 4 5 6 7 8 9 10

LIBRARY OF CONGRESS CATALOGING-IN-PUBLICATION DATA
Names: Diabaté, Massa M., author. | Auerbach, Shane, translator. | Yost, David, translator.
Title: The lieutenant of Kouta / By Massa Makan Diabate ; translated by Shane Auerbach and David Yost.
Other titles: Lieutenant de Kouta. English | African humanities and the arts.
Description: East Lansing : Michigan State University Press, 2017. | Series: African humanities and the arts |
Includes bibliographical references.
Identifiers: LCCN 2016027177| ISBN 9781611862270 (pbk. : alk. paper) | ISBN 9781609175122 (pdf) |
ISBN 9781628952834 (epub) | ISBN 9781628962833 (kindle)
Subjects: LCSH: Mali—History—Autonomy and independence movements—Fiction.
Classification: LCC PQ3989.2.D44 L513 2017 |
DDC 843/.914—dc23 LC record available at https://lccn.loc.gov/2016027177

Book design by Charlie Sharp, Sharp Des!gns, East Lansing, Michigan
Cover design and artwork by Shaun Allshouse, www.shaunallshouse.com

Michigan State University Press is a member of the Green Press Initiative and is committed to developing
and encouraging ecologically responsible publishing practices. For more information about the Green Press
Initiative and the use of recycled paper in book publishing, please visit *www.greenpressinitiative.org*.

Visit Michigan State University Press at *www.msupress.org*

Introduction

Shane Auerbach and Cheick M. Chérif Keïta

Massa Makan Diabaté has long been recognized as an important writer of the African canon. Likely Diabaté's best-known work, the 1979 *Le lieutenant de Kouta* (The lieutenant of Kouta) is the first in Diabaté's Kouta trilogy. It tells the story, part tragicomic and part hagiographic, of an African lieutenant of the French army, returning as a decorated hero from the battlefields of Europe to Kouta (a fictionalized version of Diabaté's own home of Kita, Mali). In this introduction, we present Kouta/Kita, the lieutenant, the Kouta trilogy, and Massa Makan Diabaté.

Under colonial rule since 1893, Mali (called French Sudan for the majority of the colonial era, and later, in 1958, renamed the Sudanese Republic) joined Senegal to form the Federation of Mali in 1959. The Federation of Mali gained independence from France in June 1960. By that September, Senegal had withdrawn from the federation, and the Republic of Mali was established under socialist president Modibo Keïta. *The Lieutenant of Kouta* takes us to Mali in the late 1950s, with chatter of independence increasing.

During this era, Kita was a medium-sized town that had grown as a trading and administrative center largely thanks to its positioning on the Dakar-Niger railway that connected Dakar and Bamako. Kita is also a town of great cultural significance in Mali—it is featured in epics of the oral tradition and is the birth-place of many Malian artists. Kita town was the administrative center of Kita *canton*, an agglomeration of towns for which there was a canton chief, selected from one of a few lineages. In turn, Kita canton was one of several that comprised the Kita *cercle*, again centered in Kita. Under the colonial administration, the cercle was the smallest administrative unit that was headed by a European officer, the *commandant de cercle*. The populations of Kita town and canton were about five to eight thousand and about thirty to forty thousand respectively (Hopkins 1972, 37).

Mali was then, as it is now, predominantly Muslim. Manifestations of this include the importance of the imam and Muslim elders as well as polygamy—there were up to four wives in each household. But while El Hadj Umar Tall and his Toucouleur army had successfully Islamized much of Mali, and much of West Africa, in the mid-to-late 1800s, animism persisted. A town of Kita's size and importance had a mosque and imam, but in smaller surrounding towns, *N'komo* (animist ritualists/shamans) were prevalent. Kita also had a substantial Catholic mission that predated Mali's formal colonization and persists to this day.

Underneath the macropolitics of the canton chief, the commandant, and the colonial apparatus bubbled rich micropolitics: rivalries among wives within each household, inter- and intragenerational resentments, a discord between traditionalists and progressives, between ethnicities, between religions. It is this lattice of jockeying influences, macro and micro, political and religious, during a transitionary period that made Kita so dynamic in the '50s and '60s. That dynamism forms the basis of Diabaté's Kouta trilogy, which Sangaré (1997, 5) describes as "a more-or-less complete historical tableau of traditional Mandinka, or even African, society: a diachronic vision of the political and sociocultural evolution of Mali."

Into this fray arrived Lieutenant Siriman Keita, a former *tirailleur sénégalais*. The Tirailleurs Sénégalais were a corps of colonial infantry that fought for the French army in several wars, including both world wars. Upon their retirement, many soldiers returned to their hometowns. Keïta (1985) explains that having the retired soldiers do so was of great value to the colonial administration—a European commandant could not singlehandedly manage an entire cercle, with a significant population spread across tens or hundreds of villages, many of them extremely isolated. Rather, the colonial administration required an African sub-administration that would serve effectively as its proxy. Retired soldiers, with their discipline and loyalty to France, were considered more suitable for this purpose than trained civil servants, whose education often exposed them to subversion. Retired soldiers also received pensions, an arrangement that further inclined them to be against the independence movement, which could result in the cancellation of these stipends.

The reception from the people of the villages to which the soldiers returned was more ambivalent. Despite the social prestige they carried as proxies of the colonial apparatus, they were mocked for being self-involved, brusque, and disciplined to the point of pedantry, their mannerisms contrasting jarringly with laid-back village life. Some soldiers returned with a fondness for alcohol that exposed them to further ridicule in a Muslim society that does not drink. The generation following independence joked with the retired soldiers, the educated youth mocking their French, and the archetype of the retired soldier was put to comic use in songs and other media.

The great irony of the retired soldiers is that despite their support for the colonial apparatus, they also deserve some credit for its demise. As Keïta (1985, 212) points out, "In having Africa participate in her war efforts, in defense of her liberty, how could France continue to deny the colonies the right to justice and equality? It is clear that the atmosphere created by the return of the retired soldiers from the two world wars contributed in a big way to the acceleration of the political emancipation of African nations."

While the protagonist is a retired soldier, our narrator, Diabaté, is a griot. Diabaté, born in Kita in 1938, was a descendant of a long line of *jali* (known as griots in Western terminology) and the nephew of Kélé Monson Diabaté, a griot of particular renown. The term *griot* is hard to define succinctly. Griots are the keepers of the oral tradition in a society without a written one—that is, they are the historians, journalists, and scholars of West African society. Historically, they were advisors to kings. But they are also storytellers, performance artists, and entertainers, often willing to bend the truth for entertainment purposes. Further, they fulfill the role of media, spreading both important news and salacious gossip. And just as Western media can become entangled with their subjects, with celebrities trading access for favorable coverage, some griots sing praise songs for established elites, expecting money in return.

Diabaté's upbringing was shaped by the influence of two uncles. One, Kélé Monson, trained him as a *jali*, inculcating Massa Makan with the oral tradition of the Mande. Kélé Monson was a traditionalist—he was highly critical of modern griots, accusing them of eschewing the oral tradition in favor of entertainment and rumormongering, and of singing praise songs for living elites for the sole purpose of profit. He compared them to beggars. Massa Makan would go on to share Kélé Monson's disdain for the modern griot, but not Kélé Monson's traditionalism. Juxtapose Massa Makan's training under Kélé Monson with his experiences with another uncle, Djigui Diabaté. It was under the care of Djigui that Massa Makan was schooled in Guinea. Djigui, a doctor working for the colonial services, was married to a French woman, and Massa Makan honed his French under their care. Djigui was the modern counterpoint to Kélé Monson's traditionalism, and Massa Makan's travels back and forth between the two exposed him to this duality from a young age.

At seventeen, Diabaté left Africa for France, where he studied sociology and anthropology at the Sorbonne in Paris. Upon his return to Mali, he worked at the Malian Institute of Social Studies before becoming a junior minister of information under the military regime of Moussa Traoré in the early '70s. He later settled in Abidjan, the capital of the Ivory Coast, working for UNICEF and continuing his writing.

Diabaté's early works were not novels. Rather, he took *fasa*, the epic praise songs of the oral tradition, and translated them into written French, fusing the oral tradition with a modern medium. Sangaré (1997, 15) explains that "to write, for Diabaté, was to seek external support for oral tradition, to preserve Mandinka social and cultural values, to leave an imprint of his own culture." Like a painter seeking to master a classical aesthetic before developing his own, Massa Makan apprenticed in the translation of these *fasa*. It was also a bold experiment to represent the oral tradition in writing. Sagna (2001, 277) notes the difficulty of translating *fasa* into French and lauds Massa Makan's work: "Diabaté demonstrates his competence in Maninka in the way he transposes the Maninka syntax into French. His turns of phrase truly breathe the Mandinka model of discourse; he removes almost nothing from Kélé Monson's Maninka expression." Kélé Monson was not fundamentally opposed to experimentation—part of his fame came from his weekly national radio performances of these *fasa*, itself a deviation from the traditional role of *jali*—but he was unenthused by this work. In a Radio France Internationale production (Diabaté et al. 1985), Massa Makan recalls showing one of his earlier books, *Kala Jata*, to Kélé Monson. Kélé Monson's response: "These are words that no longer breathe." In the same recording, Massa Makan admits that these translations of *fasa* were mediocre in comparison with Kélé Monson's versions.

If Diabaté sought to probe the limits of the oral tradition in representing *fasa* in written French, he betrayed that oral tradition in his decision to write novels. In Abidjan, Bernard Binlin Dadié, a renowned Ivorian poet, playwright, and novelist, encouraged Diabaté to consider writing novels, arguing that it was easier than representing *fasa* in that the novelist was not constrained by the responsibility of faithfully representing stories that were both already widely known and incredibly important to the culture. Diabaté followed that advice and wrote five novels, including the Kouta trilogy. But Diabaté's novels cannot be considered as entirely separated from the oral tradition—in fact, they reflect back upon the oral tradition, for example in their portrayals of speech and of the *fraternité de case*, a brotherhood between men who were circumcised in the same group. The lieutenant's name, Siriman Keita, brings to mind Sunjata Keita, the subject of the most important of the Mande *fasa*, the epic of Sunjata. But Siriman is not a modern Sunjata. Where Sunjata is Mali's foundational hero, Siriman is a compelling Malian antihero, a complicated, nuanced character. We might even view Siriman as a parody of Sunjata. Hess (2006) also identifies within the Kouta trilogy a desecration of traditional icons and a representation of the corruption of the oral tradition. Speaking of his novels in Diabaté et al. (1985), Massa Makan explained, "I am Kélé Monson's son, but a traitorous son."

In the realm of African literature, Diabaté's Kouta trilogy stands out for its simplicity and accessibility. While colonialism's grand injustice is evident in the trilogy, Diabaté focuses on the comedic quotidian of the colonial apparatus: flawed European administrators forming fragile alliances, hoping to further (or at least preserve) their careers. You will find in the first chapter that Diabaté's comedy is largely physical. This physical comedy, the theme of the weak outwitting the strong, and the archetype of the false believer are all defining features of *Kotéba*, traditional satirical Malian theater. The archetype of the retired soldier is itself well-developed within Malian popular culture, particularly through Idrissa Soumaoro's song "Petit (N')Imprudent (Ancien Combattant)," which was copied and popularized abroad by a Congolese artist, Zao. Many of the trilogy's characters are based on real people—Sangaré (1997) explores these connections extensively.

The Kouta trilogy combines Malian inspirations and cultural references with European ones. Diabaté was particularly interested in French medieval and

Renaissance writing, in which he saw many similarities with the Mande oral tradition. A military encounter in *The Lieutenant of Kouta* is reminiscent of both "The Picrocholine War" of Francois Rabelais's *Gargantua*, and of French filmmaker Jacques Tati's *Mr. Hulot's Holiday*. Diabaté is sometimes called the Malian Balzac, as his faithful treatment of Kita across several novels with repeating characters is analogous to Honoré de Balzac's treatment of Paris. Diabaté was cosmopolitan. Like his uncle Djigui, he married a French woman. He even named his two sons after Victor Hugo and Stéphane Mallarmé respectively.

Diabaté's writing career can be interpreted, as it is in Keïta (1995), through the lens of two forces: *fasiya* and *fadenya*. *Fasiya*, whose root is the aforementioned *fasa*, is the collective heritage into which the artist is born. It is the artist's belonging to caste and family, his birthright. It is through this *fasiya* that Massa Makan apprenticed in the oral tradition under Kélé Monson, and *fasiya* is a centripetal force in that it inspires the artist to work toward the continuation of that collective heritage into which he was born. *Fadenya* is an opposing force: it is the desire of the individual to distinguish himself from his ancestors, his father in particular, and surpass their success. A common Bambara saying holds that there are three types of sons: he who does not reach the renown of his father, he who equals it, and he who surpasses it. The notion of the father in Malian culture is broad; as is evident in the quotation of Massa Makan above, he viewed himself as the son of Kélé Monson, and it was Kélé Monson's renown that Massa Makan was driven, through the force of *fadenya*, to surpass.

Fadenya is centrifugal. Massa Makan could not surpass Kélé Monson's renown by emulating him. Instead, he wrote novels. His betrayal of the oral tradition was also his innovation, that which brought him renown. For his novels, he won the 1974 *Grand prix littéraire d'Afrique noire* of the Association of French Language Writers, and the 1987 *Grand prix international* of the Léopold Sédar Senghor Foundation.

While the rivalry inherent in *fadenya* may at first seem destructive insofar as it drives the artist away from the collective heritage, it is also constructive in that the resulting innovations can be integrated back into the collective heritage, the *fasiya*, increasing the cultural wealth. This is the case with Diabaté. He betrayed Kélé Monson and the oral tradition, but this betrayal was of immense cultural value. Because of this contribution, and despite his betrayal, he is welcomed back into the collective heritage. Two schools in Mali and an important literary award are named after him. He is widely thought of not just as a novelist, but also a griot of great importance and renown. In a sense, the already rather malleable definition of a griot expanded to encompass Diabaté.

At the very beginning of this novel, Diabaté suggests he had intended to write the novel in Maninka but ended up writing it in French out of laziness. One might imagine Diabaté, a known provocateur, winking at the reader as he teases his mentor Kélé Monson with this statement. His choice of language and medium was neither accidental nor out of laziness. Rather, he sought a broader audience. He strove not just to preserve the values of the oral tradition, but to expand upon them. Later in his life, he considered publishing directly in English. He hoped to have his novels translated. We believe he would be pleased with this publication.

NOTE

All quotations of French sources are translated by the authors of this introduction.

WORKS CITED

Diabaté, Massa M. *Kala jata*. 1970. Bamako, Mali: Éditions populaires.

———. 1979. *Le lieutenant de Kouta*. Paris: Éditions Hatier.

———. 1980. *Le coiffeur de Kouta*. Paris: Éditions Hatier.

———. 1982. *Le boucher de Kouta*. Paris: Éditions Hatier.

Diabaté, Massa M., Jean-Christophe Deberre, Drissa Diakité, and Françoise Ligier. 1985. *Massa Makan Diabaté*. Archives Sonores de la Littérature Noire. Radio France Internationale. Vinyl recording.

Hess, Deborah. 2006. *La poétique de renversement chez Maryse Condé, Massa Makan Diabaté et Édouard Glissant*. Paris: L'Harmattan.

Hopkins, Nicholas S. 1972. *Popular government in an African town: Kita, Mali*. Chicago: University of Chicago Press.

Keïta, Cheick M. Chérif. 1985. "L'évolution de la relation coloniale à travers l'image de l'ancien combattant." In *Proceedings of the Meeting of the French Colonial Historical Society*, vol. 10. East Lansing: Michigan State University Press.

———. 1995. *Massa Makan Diabaté: Un griot mandingue à la rencontre de l'écriture*. Paris: L'Harmattan.

Sagna, Karim. 2001. *Massa Makan Diabaté au carrefour de l'initiation et de l'écriture*. PhD diss., University of Arizona.

Sangaré, Mamadou. 1997. *L'histoire et le roman dans la trilogie kouta de Massa Makan Diabaté: "Le lieutenant de kouta," "le coiffeur de kouta," "le boucher de kouta."* Diss., Université Sorbonne Nouvelle—Paris 3.

Soumaoro, Idrissa. 2003. "Petit Imprudent." *Köte*. Wrasse Records. CD.

The Lieutenant
of Kouta

Principal Characters

Togoroko	*the village idiot*
Lieutenant Siriman Keita	*retired soldier*
Famakan	*the lieutenant's adopted son*
Faganda	*the lieutenant's older brother, who lives in Kouroula*
Awa	*the lieutenant's wife*
N'Godé	*a nurse at the Kouta clinic*
Solo	*a blind man and scandalmonger*
Old Soriba	*a village elder with a love for fine food*
Amy	*one of Soriba's wives*
Bertin	*colonial administrator*
Dotori	*the commandant, predecessor of Bertin*
The Imam	*religious leader of the Muslim community*
Daouda	*a wealthy storekeeper*
Leroy	*a doctor and colonel, head of the Kouta clinic before independence*
Koulou Bamba	*chief of the canton of Kouta*
Bakou	*the commandant's orderly*
Namori	*a butcher known as a miser*
Doussouba	*owner of a cheap restaurant*
N'Pé	*a witch doctor*
Bakou	*chief of the village of Woudi*

"Famakan, ite kilo ba kamio kilo?"
"Kami kili le."
"Famakan, mun dun ti ite bulo si o ma?"
"Ba lietnan . . ."
"Hun! . . ."

"Famakan, is that your egg or a guinea fowl's?"
"It's a guinea fowl egg."
"But then, Famakan, why did you take it?"
"Papa lieutenant . . ."
"Ah!"

My intention was to tell this story in Maninka.
But laziness kept me from searching out the
right word, from honing the sentence.

I.

HANDS BOUND, HEAD COVERED IN EGG YOLK, PULLED BY LIEUTENANT SIRIMAN Keita, Famakan had no idea what he had coming.

"The Whites!" the lieutenant screamed. "This is all the Whites' fault! In the old days, a child of seven years was already in the fields. Today, they want to educate them. And what an education! Monday, they sleep off the exhaustions of Sunday. Tuesday, they work a little. Wednesday, they get ready to go out on Thursday. And Friday, they start dreaming of Sunday. And the second they know how to write their names, they speak of independence.

"Independence? In other words, no more pension for the lieutenant. No more pension for all those who showed, on the other side of the sea, the courage of our race. It's nothing but jealousy! Selfishness! Well, until the day they put dirt in my ears, the jealous and envious will find me here in Kouta, as sure as the sun follows the rain."

The lieutenant drew out the whole village with his shouting.

"It would have been better, Famakan, if an eagle had taken you from your mother's back at two months old. Your punishment will be exemplary. It would have been better if your mother's pagne had come undone in the middle of the market. Everybody could have seen her *boutou-ba*[1] at their leisure! Her bushy slit. Nobody would have married her, and you would never have been born."

The women covered their ears to avoid hearing any more, saying, "Some neighbor the lieutenant is! Such insults, and on such a beautiful morning! . . . And from the mouth of a man!"

"Famakan, your parents conceived you by day. We're told over and over again not to do that during the day. The siesta has spoiled this country. The child of the siesta will never amount to anything! Such children have no right to life. In the old days, they were abandoned in a cave where they died of starvation; or the family matriarch, on the advice of the elders, performed a bleeding, and their blood drained softly, slowly, and for a long time, chasing off the evil that they bore.

"Go to a house in Kouta after lunch and ask for the father of the family. You'll be told he's taking a siesta. An improved siesta . . . Siestas make us ugly and unlucky. And the Whites have their share of the responsibility. They put thieves in prison, where they're fed. In the old days of this country, before the Whites' arrival—with their laws, their judgments, their mitigating circumstances—well, thieves had long nails pushed into their heads, softly, slowly, and for a long time. They were buried alive. They had their throats slit in the town square with badly sharpened knives, to make examples of them."

Famakan followed the lieutenant without saying a word, his eyes wild. He suddenly remembered what had happened to his classmate, Fakourou. It was the dry season; the harmattan was blowing, and the whole village had disappeared in the swirling wind. Fakourou had found a long cigarette butt at the edge of the market. On the Dotori Bridge, he saw a man smoking, snug in the old coat of an ex-soldier. Since many locals wore similar clothes, given to them by relatives who had gone to war in the white man's land, he didn't recognize the recently arrived Lieutenant Siriman Keita.

Fakourou asked the man for a light, his right temple bent forward, the cigarette butt pasted to his lips, awaiting the first, nostril-warming puff. The lieutenant had discreetly passed his cigarette from his right hand to his left. And by way of response, he gave Fakourou a slap so violent that the boy saw lights crisscrossing before his eyes! Scared out of his wits, he set off running from the Dotori Bridge to the school. He was seized by a high fever, and rumor had it that an evil spirit had beaten him.

"This village needs to be ruled with an iron fist," the lieutenant shouted, "like the Colonial Army! Until the day you die, you will never steal again. I, Lieutenant

Siriman Keita, swear it myself. At the mere glimpse of a fallen object on the ground, you will flee in panic. Ah, the Whites. There's only one thing to teach the children of siestas: he who steals an egg today will steal an ox tomorrow."

The people of the neighborhood who were eating their breakfast stopped passing bowls from father to son, from mother to daughter. All eyes followed Famakan, held by the lieutenant's leash like a dog. Egg yolk ran into his eyes. He tried to wipe his face, but at that moment, the lieutenant pulled the cord taut, and Famakan collapsed into a mud puddle.

"Get up or I'll slit your throat!" the lieutenant roared, drawing the saber he always carried on his belt.

"Kill me now," Famakan murmured, "and let's be done with it."

"Not before I judge you!" threatened the lieutenant, catching Famakan's gaze with the gleam of his saber.

They arrived at the square house, and Siriman immediately barricaded his door to keep out the crowd of onlookers that had followed him since the Dotori Bridge. Then he dragged Famakan into his living room, ordered him to sit on the floor, and bound his arm to a chair.

"Now, Famakan, let's be frank. This egg—was it you who laid it, or one of my guinea fowls?"

"Has anyone ever seen a man lay an egg?"

"Well, you're going to lay one today, and I bet it'll be big enough to hang over the mosque."

"Sir . . ."

"Call me 'Lieutenant'!" shouted Siriman. "It's my rank; I won it under fire against the enemies of France while your father and your mother were frolicking like geckos in full daylight. I myself made some female conquests overseas. After all, I am a man; I eat salt, and he who eats salt . . ."

He stopped and took on a menacing look. "And if, one day, a boy or a girl, child of some red-butted monkey, decides to come here, to Kouta, in search of his father, I'll drag him behind the village by the tree nursery and put him down with a revolver."

"Lieutenant, I took an egg from beneath a bush, it's true . . ."

"So you admit the facts. Here is my sentence, then."

"Whether it was a guinea fowl egg or a chicken egg, I'm not sure. And there's no longer any proof. You broke it on my head."

"Only guinea fowls lay their eggs under the bushes, and all of the guinea fowls in the village belong to me." The response embarrassed him, and he added: "And even if it was a chicken egg, in my eyes, you're still a thief. Your punishment will be severe, Famakan!"

He got up, looked around for a while, and finally went into his bedroom, returning with a revolver. He took a new rope from the wall and put it in a bucket of water. And to prolong Famakan's torture, the lieutenant sat down in front of him, thoughtful, his head in his hands.

"Choose between the revolver and the rope," the lieutenant finally said. "You want the revolver? Then I'll burn your face, and until the day of your death, you'll remember not to steal. The rope take your fancy? An old custom of ours! I'll beat you until it crumbles."

Famakan's anxious gaze went from the revolver to the rope, and from the rope to the lieutenant's face.

"Take your time, Famakan; I'm in no hurry. A retired soldier awaits nothing but death." He picked up the revolver. "This weapon dates back to the First World War. It has already served at Verdun. We should give it a test."

An explosion of gunpowder made the walls tremble, and Famakan understood that the lieutenant, who was reloading his weapon, was not joking.

"Papa Lieutenant," he said, sweetly.

"Don't call me 'Papa,' of all things. I have neither wife nor child. And heaven grant that I never father a son like you."

"Then I'll be honest: I don't want the revolver or the rope."

The lieutenant jumped as if he'd been stung by a wasp. "Famakan, you have a sore asshole; you need to just take a crap and get it over with. I'll go get you a third and final proposition . . ."

"A thief, Lieutenant, should die in the mud. Everyone should see him struggle for his life before expiring."

"So be it! I'm going to throw you from a bridge."

"The Dotori Bridge, Lieutenant. It's the highest in the village."

"Agreed, Famakan!"

Followed by the gawkers waiting outside his gate, the lieutenant set out, holding Famakan by the rope.

"He's suicidal," the lieutenant shouted. "He chose for me to throw him from a bridge. Let none accuse me of murder!"

Famakan knew the Dotori Bridge well. The children of the village came to splash about there during the rainy season, in the stagnant water, among the dead leaves and lilies. He knew the spot where a rock had injured him, and that farther out, there was nothing but mud and sand.

Now the lieutenant began to show some concern. "This would be too severe a punishment," he said. "Let's go back to the house."

But already the young boy had grabbed hold of the lieutenant at the very edge of the bridge.

"I want to go, but not all alone."

"Let me go, Famakan!"

They grappled like wrestlers, and the lieutenant, pulled over by Famakan, fell head-first into the mud, legs in the air. To disguise his ruse, the boy dove in after him, to the applause, shouts, and laughter of the audience.

"Mark my words," the lieutenant howled. "Whoever tells this story will have to pay twenty francs! Ten francs will go to me, and ten will go to Famakan."

The lieutenant climbed out of the mud and cleared a path through the crowd, cursing: "The Whites! . . . the Whites, and nothing but the Whites! They spoiled this country. It needs to be ruled with an iron fist, like the Colonial Army."

2.

Lieutenant Siriman Keita was from the village of Kouroula, twenty kilometers from Kouta. The old men swear that on his first day at the school for the sons of chiefs, he came dressed in panther skins, riding a saddled and bridled horse, while a pack of griots chanted praise songs in his family's honor. In the classroom, his father, then the chief of the whole canton, had ordered a miniature throne erected, to be surrounded by servants armed with flyswatters. The commandant gave strict orders to the young teacher from William-Ponty, where African officials were trained:

"Don't call on young Siriman Keita unless he raises his hand."

The scandalmongering in our country? A nuisance, I agree. But the old men, who keep the memories of the past, report that Siriman didn't raise his hand until six years later. His father, stripped of his position by a Corsican administrator in favor of a distant cousin, advised Siriman to enlist in the Colonial Army. He was sent to Kanta, near Darako, the colonial capital, and a few years later to Fréjus, and he fought gallantly wherever the French presence was threatened.

Since his retirement, he lived in Kouta in a big square house, twenty-five by twenty-five meters, surrounded by an imposing court of relatives and sycophants. Each had a well-defined task. One was to go early in the morning to choose the best pieces of meat; another was charged with keeping the house stocked with red wine because, as the lieutenant often said, "Never eat without giving your meal the extra flavor of a good glass of wine." He had had the square house constructed before his retirement. This had been the subject of much discussion in Kouta when the masons, assisted by all the town's prisoners, began building it without the least explanation. They'd received a blueprint and precise instructions from the commandant.

"The house must be square, with a double gate and no other entrance."

The people of Kouta had several theories, notably this one:

"With this outbreak of new ideas, maybe the commandant's building a new prison with an eye to more arrests?"

The day before the lieutenant's arrival, Commandant Dotori had asked the town crier to announce the arrival of a worthy son of the nation, a great contributor to the French cause, arriving on the ten o'clock train and meriting a welcome of balafons, tabors, and talking drums.

Lieutenant Siriman Keita stepped down from the car reserved for government officials; six steps from the commandant, he snapped to attention and froze there as if petrified. The cercle guards played "La Marseillaise," and the schoolchildren sang it. Then the players of the balafon, tabor, and talking drum gave their imaginations free rein.

A song was born, which became the lieutenant's praise song:

Lieutenant Siriman Keita,
Child of our country,
You went to the land of the Whites.
You carried the rifle for them.
We will follow your example.

Wedged into the official car, to the right of the commandant, the lieutenant came to the house, where a reception was held to celebrate his return to his native land. In full ceremonial dress, covered with all his medals, he chatted with his host.

"You know, Lieutenant, there's a wave of protest against France. It concerns us greatly. There's talk of independence."

"We must crush it, Commandant. We must crack down without mercy," the lieutenant advised.

"But what will France's age-old enemies say?"

"France's enemies? To hell with them, Commandant! France concerns herself only with her friends."

"Well said, Lieutenant. Clearly I can rely on you to explain to the people that independence would be but a delusion, a mirage."

"If I were the canton chief . . ."

Commandant Dotori was expecting this question. He knew that Siriman had come to Kouta to seek the chiefdom, and that his relationship with Faganda, his half-brother, was strained over their inheritance, and that that was why he'd preferred to build his home in Kouta. Dotori took a moment to prepare his response.

"You, boy, we're dying of thirst over here. Don't forget that Lieutenant Siriman Keita is the guest of honor."

The server brought two flutes of champagne.

"Commandant," the lieutenant said, "I've kept simple tastes. A glass of red wine will quench my thirst."

"You're right, Lieutenant. Champagne puts us to sleep, and red wine awakens our blood. To your health, Lieutenant!"

"To the Colonial Army, my friend! Good Lord, to the Colonial Army!"

"Well, then, to the Colonial Army!" the commandant repeated, stifling a laugh.

"Independence," the lieutenant huffed, wiping his lips with the back of his hand. "Given what's coming, you're going to need partners who won't hesitate to strike, even at risk of losing their own popularity."

Dotori set his glass down; he had barely wet his lips.

"Another glass, Lieutenant," he said.

The server brought the bottle of red wine.

"Put it there on the table," Dotori said. "The lieutenant will help himself, and I can empathize; with all the smoke on these trains, he needs to wash his throat."

The lieutenant filled his glass and emptied it in one gulp, smiling blissfully, his eyes dilated. The commandant had prepared his response; it was neither a refusal nor a commitment. A refusal would have left him no chance of working with the lieutenant; and if the commandant had made a promise, Siriman would have mentioned it to somebody in confidence, and gossip would have carried it to the elderly canton chief. Dotori knew Africa too well to make that mistake.

"I know that your family has often held the chiefdom. Obviously the colonial administrator always intervenes, but discreetly. His role is to act as a pacifier." He stopped and took a sip from his glass. "You see, when I received the order to build a house for you in Kouta, because you didn't want to return to your native village of Kouroula, I told myself: here's the man for the job. What's more, your superior officer sent me a confidential letter concerning you. What praise, Lieutenant, what praise!"

He signaled the server, who hurried over to refill the lieutenant's glass.

"Koulou Bamba is still effective. But he's getting old, which handicaps his decision making. Be patient, Lieutenant, and we'll do great things together."

Dotori leaned over to the lieutenant and whispered, "To succeed a chief, or to have influence over him, marry one of his daughters."

The two men burst into laughter.

"Now let's leave our guests to eat and drink, and go to see your house. Naturally, if there's any detail not to your taste, the builders will fix it."

Lieutenant Siriman Keita surveyed the property. He couldn't hide his admiration for this house: its squareness, its whiteness, the thick wall that surrounded it, and the way it towered over the village.

"Commandant, you chose the spot so well! It's exactly as I'd imagined it."

"Obviously, the money wasn't quite enough."

"Well, then . . ."

"No, Lieutenant, you owe nothing. I gave orders to the cercle's accountant." He shrugged his shoulders and gestured evasively.

"I have to use my slush fund somehow, or the governor will take it away."

"You're too kind, Commandant."

"Come now! One's never too kind to one's friends."

3.

Few people, other than relatives from Kouroula, were invited to the square house, and few people from Kouta would have accepted an invitation. In the evenings, surrounded by his court, the lieutenant recounted his military exploits in great detail.

"As much as you hate the hare, you have to admit he can run. Well, friends, the Krauts are courageous men. They follow orders without complaint, and you have to admit that retreat is not one of their tactics. One column mounts an attack, and another is positioned behind, with orders to fire on those who retreat. When the first column has endured enough losses, it's immediately relieved by the second. And so they advance to their final objective."

Every so often, he raised his glass:

"Let's drink our fill, for we are among the wealthy."

The court repeated in chorus:

"Let's drink our fill, for we are among the wealthy."

"Ranks like lieutenant, commander, and even general, these are nothing but bureaucratic promotions. And it's all who you know; you can be a commander without ever seeing battle. But the Croix de Guerre!"

"Do tell, Lieutenant."

And the lieutenant gave another recital of the story, quite different from that of the day before.

"The Krauts had caught us by surprise, throwing their first and second columns against us. They'd gotten orders to take our position and 'clean' it. Do you know what it means to 'clean' a position?"

"No!"

"To clean a position, it means to capture and kill all those who are defending it, to take no prisoners."

"Because the prisoners, they slow down the march."

"That's it exactly; you talk as if you were there. All day long we traded fire. Men fell on both sides. The next day, I realized that I held the highest rank of all of the survivors. Neither side had any ammunition left, so I ordered a bayonet attack. Carnage, my friends. It's a shame that there aren't any vultures in the land of the Whites, because that day we would have treated them to a feast. Another unit was informed of our situation by radio and came to our aid."

"'Who ordered this assault?' the colonel asked.

"'I, Second Lieutenant Siriman Keita, serial number 7577.'

"'And why, Lieutenant?'

"'If the Krauts mounted such an effective surprise attack against us, our position must have strategic value.'

"'Good! You're a good soldier. I'll inform the general of your success.'

"And that's how in a single day I was promoted to lieutenant and awarded the Croix de Guerre."

When he was feeling light-hearted, the lieutenant sometimes ventured into a story of romantic conquest, without ever finishing it.

"I was in a bistro—that is, a place where you buy wine on condition of drinking it on-site. A woman was facing me; she showed so much of herself that I lowered my head in shame. If you see up to a woman's thigh, you can easily guess the rest; even the village idiot knows that beyond the hill, there is a plain. When I least expected it, she came to me. She put her mouth in mine. She pressed me like a boa constrictor. But look out! Hey now!... Her hands were in the pockets of my jacket, going deeper and deeper. Looking for my money. And as it was the morning—and one must never do that during the day—I said no when she invited me to her house. She was a truly bad woman."

He stopped, leaving his audience unsatisfied.
"Let's drink our fill . . ."
And the courtiers chimed in:
"For we are among the wealthy."

4.

Lieutenant Siriman Keita came to market sometimes in full dress uniform, escorted closely by courtiers who cleared the children from his path. The men rose, removed their hats, and saluted him.

"Good day, Lieutenant."

He pretended not to see them, examining the produce arrayed on the stands, reprimanding a woman whose baobab leaves had not been washed. The butcher feared these impromptu visits and ordered his apprentices to clean the tables before the lieutenant reached them. And there were always the same insults:

"Dogs come to prowl your shop at night!" the lieutenant raged. "I hear them tearing each other apart. You'll give rabies to the entire village. Murderer!"

"But I can't stay up all night, Lieutenant."

"You're rich enough to afford a watchman."

"Very expensive, Lieutenant. Too expensive."

"In that case, I'll lend some money to one of my relatives, and he'll come set up shop here as a butcher."

The inspection complete, he returned to his house, avoiding the mosque, where the elders would already be blathering back and forth.

"To go to the mosque," he would tell himself, "that is fine. But if you linger there, that means you're being hounded by some relentless creditors. To think that I'll have to command over such people."

After midnight, when all his courtiers were sleeping, he stretched out before his gate, his rifle loaded with rock salt for the inevitable thief. Often he shot at dogs, for the simple pleasure of making noise. It was said in Kouta that he couldn't get to sleep without the scent of gunpowder.

He was also seen at balafon concerts, when the full moon spread over the village. His arrival was announced by whispering; the balafonist played the lieutenant's praise song, striking his instrument with all his might:

Lieutenant Siriman Keita,
Child of our country,
You went to the land of the Whites.
You carried the rifle for them . . .

The women took up the song in chorus, and the lieutenant stood right in the middle of the circle, happy to be recognized. His courtiers massaged his legs and lifted his arms. Women twirling around him, he took out his wallet and, without counting them, dropped bills on the balafon player. His audience satisfied, Siriman Keita returned home, relaxed and pleased with his own importance.

■　　■　　■

The lieutenant's tranquility was disturbed by Faganda's frequent visits, particularly after harvests, when Faganda had to contact various traders and get an idea of the going prices.

Faganda was the lieutenant's older brother. The two men had opposing temperaments: where the lieutenant knew how to forgive, recognize his mistakes, and laugh at himself, Faganda was authoritarian, suspicious, and obsessed with his family's glorious past.

"God has given me many qualities," he said. "But there's only one I don't like: I don't know how to forget when someone's wronged me."

The lieutenant deferred to him, hurried at his call, said yes to his every wish, and lowered his voice when talking to him.

When a courtier asked a question:

"I'm only the manager of this house," Siriman said. "Speak to the owner."

Faganda then made his ruling, without appeal. The lieutenant acquiesced.

He dreaded evenings in his brother's company and went more often to the balafon concerts. When the lieutenant stayed in, the evenings always ended in shouting and threats.

"Let's drink our fill," said Faganda.

"For we are among the wealthy," replied the courtiers.

By the fifth glass, Faganda launched into incoherent rants that only the lieutenant understood.

"The womb unites, the phallus divides."

Then he let his old grudges take over.

"That, I will never forget!" he set off, furious. "You chose the commandant to build your house. So my enemies all said: 'They're not from the same mother!' That's what they said: 'He doesn't trust his brother. If he sets up in Kouta, it's because he wants to avoid him.' That's what my enemies in Kouroula said. In Kouta, they call me 'Siriman's brother.'"

The lieutenant let the storm pass and tried to explain the same as always:

"Military regulation requires each colonial soldier to call on the commandant to have a house built."

"Fine! But why Kouta?"

" . . ."

"Answer me! Why did you have it built in Kouta instead of returning to Kouroula to live with us? Because Kouta is the capital of the cercle?"

" . . ."

"Because we're nothing but a bunch of farmers. Lieutenant Siriman Keita would have lacked his comforts in Kouroula among the farmers. He needs to live in Kouta, the capital of the cercle."

" . . ."

"And why didn't you write to tell me that you were moving to Kouta? Why?"

" . . ."

He'd had his fill of wine, and the lieutenant knew that further discussion with Faganda was useless when this almost womanly jealousy seized him and made him aggressive.

"Siriman, you're a bad brother and a selfish person. Ask me why."

"Why?"

"Your pension, your only source of income, isn't guaranteed. I found this out: if you die, it'll be canceled. You need to take a wife so she inherits it and the family keeps making money."

The lieutenant lowered his head, visibly ill at ease.

"That's good advice. I'll let you know as soon as my choice is made."

"'Your choice'? You said 'your choice'?" Faganda picked up his walking stick, a menacing look on his face. "I've chosen for you."

"Listen, Faganda, I'd like to marry a daughter of the canton chief. This alliance would erase a lot of bad blood."

"No!" Faganda raged. "You're not going to marry a daughter of the man who conspired with Commandant Dotori and our enemies to rob us of the chiefdom."

He threw his glass at the wall, shattering it.

"The lieutenant's brother has had his share of pain and sorrow for the evening."

5.

THE LIEUTENANT HAD SEEN HER AT MARKET, NEAR THE BUTCHER'S. SHE HELD herself apart from the women who pushed, flailed, and insulted each other, each wanting to be served before the others to get the best pieces. She was dressed in a boubou of violet bazin, half-covered by a pagne with green and yellow stripes. An indigo-dyed cotton kerchief hung from her head. She wore bracelets of thick silver on her wrists, signifying that she was neither married nor engaged. Gemstone earrings swayed with the movements of her head. A large filigreed necklace threw shimmers of gold over her bronze skin. Her features were regular, her nose straight. Only her strong lips betrayed her mixed Mandinka and Fula origins. Her nonchalant, distant attitude conveyed the elegance of a high-caste woman.

The butcher gave her a big smile of admiration and respect. She returned it, bowing her head.

The lieutenant said to himself: "Don't choose your wife from a distance, nor on a day of celebration." On the pretext of ordering a leg of lamb, he approached the butcher and could see that she was very beautiful, perhaps a bit young.

"She's the fourth daughter of the canton chief," said the butcher, preempting the lieutenant's question. "She grew up with the chief's older brother, the head of Darako Station."

"Her name?" the lieutenant whispered.

"Sira. I cut myself one day, watching her."

"Enough!" the lieutenant grumbled. "I've never had a taste for details."

From that day on, the lieutenant's appearances at the market became more frequent. He showed particular care for his appearance. It was no longer his ex-soldier's uniform that commanded respect, but a white khaki suit with golden buttons in place of medals. One morning, passing close to Sira, he gave her a coin.

"My girl, buy a kola nut for your father on my behalf."

Stunned, she hesitated.

"I've failed in my duty to greet the chief since my arrival in Kouta. We retired soldiers need time to come back to the bosom of tradition."

She smiled and closed her hand. The lieutenant saw that she had perfectly white teeth.

That very evening, Lieutenant Siriman Keita went to the house of the elderly canton chief on the pretext of asking after his health.

"I heard a rumor that you were suffering," he said.

"My rheumatism sparks up at the beginning of the wet season," replied the chief.

"Yes, the storks are returning," the lieutenant confirmed, "and the sky's already heavy with large clouds."

He paused and then said in a joking tone:

"I usually calm mine down by rubbing my joints with salted shea butter."

"What are you saying?" the chief scolded. "You aren't even fifty."

"Soon I'll be forty-five, if I'm to believe the birth date in my army record. You forget that I served fifteen years in the army."

"Forty-five!" the chief said with disgust. "At that age, I rode the world at the speed of a stallion."

The lieutenant told himself that his goal was in his sights. Every morning, after having inspected the market's cleanliness and scolded the butcher, he came to chat with the canton chief, without ever revealing his intentions.

One morning, instead of Siriman Keita coming to keep him company and chat about his pains, the chief received a messenger bearing ten kola nuts.

"We saw something in your home that pleases us."

"My blood is beautiful!" the old chief yelled with immense pride. "The

Mandinka and the Fula, traditional enemies, blend admirably. And I set the example. One carries beauty, and the other strength. The Mandinka weakens the treachery of the Fula with a touch of honesty; the Fula corrects the Mandinka's brutality with refinement. I've never stopped saying it: 'Mandinka, assimilate the Fula of the cercle through marriage.'"

He undid the package, took a kola nut, and bit into it with a crunch. Then he called his younger brother.

"From Lieutenant Siriman Keita, who covets the hand of Sira."

"We shall consider it," his younger brother said.

"If it pleases God," said the chief.

"If it pleases God," repeated the messenger.

. . .

It was the day before Bastille Day. The cercle guards passed through the village, brandishing lit torches to the sound of a brass band. They stopped before the government building and saluted them with music. Each official gave according to his means. At the square house, the guards played military marches and the lieutenant's praise song; he enjoyed listening to them, offering each guard a glass of red wine and taking out his wallet.

"Here is your gift for the holiday," he said. "We'll meet again tomorrow in the parade."

The highest-ranked grabbed a thousand-franc note, showed it to his companions, and pinned it to his shirt beside some other bills. And the orchestra headed off toward the commandant's house, followed by all the children of the village.

"The old chief's attitude surprises me," the lieutenant said to his courtiers. "I risked mentioning independence to know his feelings. And you know what he said? He told me that he, our canton chief, belonged to the past, and that independence was like a well-planted tree, and that neither the commandant nor the traditional authorities could uproot it."

He took his glass and emptied it in one gulp.

"And his enigmatic response about his daughter's marriage tells me nothing of value. A chief who can't make decisions in his own family can't make them for the canton, either."

"You need to work on his wife," said a courtier. "The crocodile tells himself that he's the king of the river. He takes an arm, rips off a leg, and everybody fears him. But in the deeper water lives the hippopotamus, who appears only to take a breath. The mother is the hippopotamus of the family. The uncles and the father boast: 'We have decided that our daughter will marry so-and-so.' No! The mother's mouth is always closest to the daughter's ear."

"The wife?" another interrupted. "What nonsense! Show a woman a real man and a drummer. Well, I guarantee, and I'd bet money on this, she'll go for the drummer. The griots, they're the ones who have all the luck with women, because they know how to say what women want to hear. How clever they are! They marry only women of their own caste—women who are immune to seduction."

"And how do you convince a mother?" the lieutenant asked. He held out his arms wide, taking the sky for his witness. "By gifts? By flaunting my wealth?"

"Of course not, Lieutenant!" exclaimed a third. "To marry a girl, you have to dazzle her mother."

"But how?" the lieutenant asked anxiously.

"If I knew that, all the girls of Kouta would be at my feet." He took a moment, then added: "In certain countries, the future mother-in-law personally tests the virility of the man who wishes to marry her daughter. And once dazzled . . ."

"Insanity!" the lieutenant shouted. "Don't speak another word of this in my house, or I'll be obliged to forbid you entry. I feed you, I shelter you, you even have the right to shit in my latrine, and you allow yourself this insolence."

"My mouth is full of dog droppings," the courtier said by way of apology. "My tongue betrayed my thought. I meant that God himself doesn't quite understand women; at a particular moment, he turned his head when he was shaping her, so as not to see there too clearly."

The lieutenant stifled an amused cough.

"Surely when he had to make the bushy slit," he said.

The courtiers burst into loud, forced laughter.

■   ■   ■

As was the custom, it was Lieutenant Siriman Keita who led the parade of cercle guards and ex-soldiers, who were covered in medals and faded decorations and dressed in patched-up rags. When everyone had assembled on the plaza, not far from the commandant's house, the lieutenant appeared in full dress uniform, caracoling his richly caparisoned horse. He gave strict orders, as if addressing real soldiers. Then he climbed off his horse and went to stand at attention before the commandant, facing the grandstand where the functionaries and the notables were seated.

"On your order, Commandant!" he said.

He ordered the troops forward for inspection, presenting the recently retired soldiers, who squared themselves in their uniforms and proudly displayed their brand new decorations. The commandant allowed himself an amused smile as he passed before this motley group of men and outfits, shaking each hand extended to him and lingering to chat with an invalid supported by a cane.

The inspection finished, the lieutenant remounted his horse, drew his sword, and simulated an attack, a pursuit, and a charge to the clamor of the crowd, lost in a whirlwind of yellow dust. Balafonists and drummers saluted his skill by playing his praise song.

"On my command!" he cried.

A bugle call resounded. In rows of three, the brass band at the head, the retired soldiers and cercle guards set off toward the Dotori Bridge. They made the rounds of the village, firing their rifles, followed by schoolchildren singing "La Marseillaise."

After the parade, the congratulations, and the reception, the lieutenant remounted his horse and, preceded by the band, set off toward the house of the old canton chief, whose crippling rheumatism had prevented him from joining the festivities. Koulou Bamba came out with all of his family to acknowledge the honor that Siriman Keita was showing him, and gave a thousand francs to the bandleader. The band began to play military anthems, and the lieutenant, to dazzle his future in-laws, turned his attention to horsemanship, making his horse kick and leap. Emboldened by the applause, at the limit of his self-control, he made his horse rear until it was almost vertical; then he ordered it to prostrate itself before his future in-laws. The beast bent its knees; the cries of admiration rose, and the band resumed, even more beautifully. Surprised, the horse reared, launching its rider into a mud-filled ditch. The crowd gathered around the lieutenant in a circle to block him from sight. The rumor spread throughout the village; his image was tarnished.

"It looks like he pooped his pants, like a baby," some said. The more merciful maintained that he had only pissed himself. The lieutenant barricaded himself in his house; several courtiers left him, some exhausted by his fits of anger, others frustrated by his reduced lifestyle.

He cut an opening in his wall, and any wandering sheep or goats that entered the square house had their throats slit with great ceremony:

"On my order! Pin the goat."

"The goat is pinned, Lieutenant."

"On my order! Cut the throat."

"The throat is cut, Lieutenant."

6.

Famakan couldn't resist the temptation to search under bushes in hope of finding more eggs. But before doing so, he carefully searched the surroundings to make sure that the lieutenant wasn't hiding behind another bush, watching out for him.

After a week, instead of one egg, he discovered two, or even three, in the same place.

"So much for the proverb that the guinea fowl never drops its eggs in the same basket," he told himself.

Every morning, his breakfast was guaranteed. He took the eggs, returned to the market, and cooked them on the embers maintained by the sellers of porridge and millet cakes. He ate one or two eggs and kept the third for Birama, who protected him against the tyranny of older children. Then he took a path through the brambles so as not to pass by the square house. And again in the same place, he found, as if on display, a brand new ten franc coin gleaming in the morning sun. When it kept happening, Famakan became quite scared; hadn't his grandmother said that some evil spirits used this trick to make contact with humans, to put them under a spell?

"To hell with these eggs and coins," he told himself.

He abstained from taking them for a week. His schoolmaster, who had complimented Famakan's quick-wittedness and attention to his studies, noticed a new laziness in him. Irritated by the distraught and lifeless eyes the boy turned to the chalkboard, the schoolmaster began beating him as he did the other students. When Famakan reported to Birama that a bigger boy had been harassing him, the other boy replied, "No egg, no protection."

In the evenings, the boys had to work in the school garden, watering seedlings and pulling weeds under the watch of the older children. They noticed that Famakan's section was less well kept, and that after selling the lettuce, cauliflower, and carrots, he always claimed to have lost ten francs. They therefore whipped him with a switch.

So Famakan went back to the little trail through the brush, which passed far from the lieutenant's house. A miracle! Under the same bush, he found a little sack surrounded by seven eggs. Famakan took only one of them for his breakfast. As for the sack, he didn't want to know what was inside.

And the next morning, when he returned to the bush, to his great surprise, the egg had been replaced. He took two of them, and brought one to Birama.

The following day, Famakan saw two little sacks under the bush, surrounded by fourteen eggs. And since Birama had demanded back pay, Famakan took them and put them in his school bag, while a burst of laughter came from a nearby bush. Famakan wanted to run, but his legs refused to obey, as if paralyzed. He felt a hand rest gently on his shoulder.

"Famakan, these eggs—was it you who laid them?" The lieutenant was there before him, considering him gravely. "Only the guinea fowls lay their eggs behind the bushes," he said, "and all of the guinea fowls belong to me."

Famakan wanted to speak, to clear his name, to make any kind of excuse, but his tongue was glued to his palate. He was suffocating with fear and anguish.

"I'm going to throw you in an abandoned well, very far from the village."

Famakan gave the lieutenant a worried look, and found that the man's face was smiling and playful.

"Have you ever eaten mayonnaise?" the lieutenant asked.

"No!"

"Well, we need peanut oil, eggs—only the yolks—salt, and onions. Only an honest man can make a good mayonnaise. At noon, when you finish school, come to the square house. I'm going to make it right before your eyes."

He lowered and turned his head, and said in an amused tone:

"You'll take a ten franc coin from one of the little sacks to buy a loaf of bread. Mayonnaise is eaten with bread."

. . .

The imam's eyes were wide with astonishment. Siriman Keita, adopting a child?

When a messenger came to him, saying that the lieutenant wished to speak about a serious matter, the imam hadn't been able to hide his worry. Since the lieutenant's arrival in Kouta, the two men hadn't had the least contact. The lieutenant hadn't even taken the trouble, as was customary, to come introduce himself and acknowledge the imam as the spiritual leader of the Muslim community. On the contrary, the lieutenant criticized believers, accused them of laziness, and blasphemed in public.

When the muezzin climbed up the minaret for the call to prayer, the lieutenant imitated him, turning his back to the mosque:

There he is again
On the highest of our terraces
Strike him and make him come down!
So great is Allah! Is Allah so great?
Then we can see him
Without climbing out on a terrace.

In Kouta, no one could boast of seeing the lieutenant at a baptism or marriage, much less a funeral.

"Me, Lieutenant Siriman Keita, attending baptisms for children conceived during the siesta? Never!" he said in public. "And why bother marrying the young when they've already been fornicating as freely as dogs? And as for their deaths, the earth, if she could decide, would surely refuse to eat such filth."

"Siriman," the imam said, "adopting a child is a serious decision. Take another week to reflect, or even a month."

"I've already reflected, and my decision is irrevocable. I want Famakan Bérété for my son. I've already spoken with the commandant, and he said it was a matter for the religious authorities."

"Famakan being fatherless, it would be preferable for you to marry his mother."

"I won't let you meddle in my love life. I want a son, not a wife. Tell me what I need to do to satisfy tradition."

"You don't belong to the great Muslim community, and I'm not authorized by the Holy Scripture to help you with your problems. But if you were to pray, even once, and in public, I could affirm that you're a Muslim."

"This is hypocrisy. You're holding a knife to my throat."

"I apply the law, Lieutenant."

"Then I will appear this week at the Friday prayer."

"God be praised!"

All of Kouta's Muslims were assembled in the square before the mosque waiting for the imam when the lieutenant arrived, draped in an embroidered boubou that a tailor had sewn in great haste, at the cost of a night's sleep. His oversized Moroccan babouches dragged in the dirt, kicking up a yellow dust. A murmur ran through the crowd:

"Have you ever seen a hyena in broad daylight?"

"It's possible. But a hyena under a mosquito net? Never!"

The lieutenant pretended not to hear their mocking and made his way through the crowd, shaking hands as he went, his face lit with an awkward, ironic smile. He went to sit at the back and unfolded a prayer mat that he'd bought that very morning. Some of the curious turned to look, smiling at him and saluting him with a nod. The lieutenant responded with a furtive wink.

"This is very good, Lieutenant," said his closest neighbor.

Siriman Keita smiled spitefully, his boubou spread out around him, his hands joined on his knees. Murmured litanies floated back to him, persistent and incomprehensible. A laugh teased his lips; he mastered it with an expression of disgust. After some *talibé* recited a few Koranic verses, the imam was announced. As soon as he saw the lieutenant, a smile of victory adorned his face. He shook the lieutenant's hand.

"I kept my word," the lieutenant said.

"I will keep mine, by the grace of God," the imam replied.

He led the prayer and then asked all the faithful to give him their attention.

"People come to Islam by different paths, and all are commendable. Lieutenant Siriman Keita has come to us, driven by a laudable desire. He wishes to adopt Famakan Bérété, a fatherless child, and by his presence among you, he asks for your acceptance. If anyone can tell me that this adoption is illegal, invoking a verse of the Koran or a tradition of our community, let him speak now before I commit an error for which he will share the responsibility."

"The Prophet himself adopted a son," said Old Soriba.

"This is the truth," the imam confirmed. "Does anyone have an objection?" The faithful shook their heads.

"Siriman Keita, come here!" said the imam.

The lieutenant stood and walked slowly toward the imam. He had lost his composure; his face showed a mixture of worry and immense joy. His legs trembled, and he lowered his head like a child fearing the reprimand of his father.

"The great Muslim community gathered here gives you Famakan Bérété for your son," the imam emphasized ceremoniously. "But never forget this: children belong to those who make them better."

He took the lieutenant by the hand and led him into the mosque.

"Give this child a mother; his happiness will be complete, and your good deed will be doubled."

. . .

"It was a setup!" the lieutenant shouted. "A setup! What am I saying, a setup? It's an uppercut. A set-uppercut. Someone even said: 'Have you ever seen a hyena under a mosquito net?' You want Famakan? Well then, come to the mosque for Friday prayer. And now, they want to put a wife in my bed. It's a set-uppercut. Well, they won't get me. I put just one foot on a prayer mat, and already they see me sitting from morning to night in the shade of the mosque, blind with admiration for a marabout reading the Koran."

He remembered the morning of Bastille Day, when his horse had thrown him right in front of the house of his future father-in-law. He felt an anger in the pit of his stomach.

All of his misfortunes stemmed from that incident. Day and night, it haunted him and kept him awake. And when his burning mind gave way to sleep, he dreamed of it.

"And I will make Famakan a skilled horseman, able to charge up to a house and carry a woman away. Even if, after the abduction, he should ask for her parents' consent."

He picked up his glass; it was the seventh he'd drunk, one after another.

"Let's drink our fill . . ."

"For we are among the wealthy," said the courtiers.

"Famakan is my son just as much as if I'd impregnated his mother on a night of leave. Notice that I said a night!"

He gave a big laugh; the courtiers followed suit.

"You all, I house you, I feed you, and when, because you've overeaten, you have diarrhea . . ."

Someone realized that the lieutenant was about to say something crude and lifted his glass:

"Let's drink our fill!"

"For we are among the wealthy," the lieutenant said mechanically.

He stood up, towering over his court with his full height:

"From this day forward, I grant Famakan command of the square house, and let whoever crosses his will take leave of us."

"Let's drink our fill!" one of the courtiers cried.

"Yes," the lieutenant replied, "to celebrate the adoption of Famakan, we'll drink a glass, and as far as I'm concerned, it will be the last, forever."

And as of that day, half of his courtiers left him.

1.

"She's a city girl," it was said in Kouta. "She's probably swallowed many a fortune and started in on still more. A hussy, that's what she is. To marry such a woman would be like seeing a stake and then sticking your eye into it."

Each morning, Awa appeared at market when it was full to bursting. The store owners had opened their doors, the sewing machines of the tailors were clicking away, and the women were loudly advertising their wares, broadcasting far and wide that the market was in full swing.

Awa took the main path to make herself conspicuous, stopping here and there, peppering her conversation with words in Wolof. Then she turned and retraced her steps, her silver bracelets clicking to the rhythm of her balanced gait.

Only the butcher claimed to be immune to this vision and the scent of perfume and incense that trailed in her wake.

"The butt?" he exclaimed. "It's just meat. It's just a haunch made for sitting down and relieving yourself."

The elders, who were chattering in the shade of the mosque, had taken exception to her and responded tersely to her greetings, insulting her with their looks.

"That woman dresses not to cover her figure, but to display it," old Birama said. And he added self-righteously: "It's written that the end of the world is coming when women behave like that."

Old Soriba didn't share the scorn that the other elders cast on Awa. "It's often said: Old Soriba is a lover. He loves women like others love meat or sugar. And I don't disagree with the Prophet, who had no disdain for them. And my father advised me: 'Soriba, if you father a boy that doesn't like women, kill him; he'll bring you no glory.' That's what he said, my father, whenever he saw me with a girl."

"We know," Birama snickered. "You've married four of them and divorced another because you wore her out."

"Nobody here can say that I didn't respect the customs prescribed by our religion in divorcing her."

"It's said," Solo joked, "that you prowl around Awa's neighborhood at night." Old Soriba stroked his beard, licking his lips as if savoring a sweet aftertaste.

"It's the music they play that gets me."

"Soriba," Birama replied, "Awa is a crocodile, and if the crocodile takes you . . ."

"I know, you find no one to pity you. If it's morning, a friend will say: 'What was he doing on the riverbank so early?' In the afternoon? A false brother like you will go around the village saying: 'What reason is there to prowl the riverbank at midday?' At night? Then one's enemies—may God provide them, Birama, they're as essential as salt—well then, the enemies will laugh: 'You'd have to be crazy to bathe at night.' I, Old Soriba, admit it myself: all Kouta says that I love women, and it's the truth. And, well, I've avoided Awa since the first day I saw her. I only like the music there, just like the Prophet, may his name be venerated."

"To love women is no vice," the imam said.

Old Soriba smiled, reassured by the support the religious leader had given him.

"Yes, God made me love women!" he cried, his face triumphant. "And he has never deprived me of them."

The imam, who generally stood on his dignity when such subjects came up, put an end to the conversation by changing the subject:

"The mosque is falling apart," he said, pointing to a gecko crawling out of a crack. "It's time to whitewash it. Perhaps we should take up a collection for it next Friday."

For almost a month, the lieutenant had dedicated himself to a curious task. He'd discovered a pair of binoculars in one of his old tin trunks and used them to follow the bustle of the market. Most of the time, he aimed his gaze at Awa.

"What a backside!" he said to himself. "No, there's something suspicious about it. God is generous, but he can't give all that to just one woman. No, it's a trick. It's a setup, like the cabaret girls in the good old days of the Colonial Army. You pay, you wait. All of your blood rushes to your leaping heart. And they take forever to undress. Once they're nude, you're seized with disappointment by their motley getup: bra, stockings, fake tits and ass, and all of it smelling of rubber. The beautiful Awa is a woman of the market, and everything at the market is for sale. But you should never buy a hat before trying it on."

The lieutenant started sending small gifts to Awa with the help of Fadiala, his most devoted courtier: a bracelet of carved ivory, a ring of silver filigree . . .

"How did she react?" he asked each time.

"Very well, Lieutenant."

"Very well—that's no answer. I want details."

"She held out both hands in a sign of respect and joy; she took off the ring that she had been wearing and replaced it on the spot with the one you offered her."

The word *respect* went straight to the lieutenant's heart. His face lit up with a smile of pure joy, his nostrils flared, and he twirled around as if attacked by ants.

Suddenly, he was seized by anxiety and stared distrustfully at Fadiala.

"Don't trick me!" he threatened, his forehead creased, his eyes narrowed. "You know better than anyone how much I've suffered since I fell from my horse."

"May lightning cleave me in two if I lie to you!"

"To hear and to see are two different things," said the lieutenant, still suspicious.

"Yes, it's time that you made your intentions known to everyone. Why don't you send her a mutton leg and have her prepare a feast for you?"

"No, here's a thousand francs," the lieutenant said. "It's fish that shows a woman's culinary talents."

At nightfall, the lieutenant arrived at Awa's house with much fanfare, followed by all his court. He ate very little, only a few scraps, each accompanied by a well-crafted compliment.

"Surely, Awa, you lived in Senegal, or more precisely, Saint-Louis."

"How did you know that?"

"By the way you cook fish. I spent two years garrisoned in that town. Well, nobody makes better fish than the people of Saint-Louis."

"But you've hardly eaten anything."

"I could have finished the platter myself. But because my companions paid such great homage to your cooking, I restrained myself. They've never eaten fish cooked the way only Saint-Louisians know how."

After the meal and the burping, each paid compliments to Awa.

"I almost bit my own hand," said Fadiala.

Somebody risked a joke:

"A well-seasoned dish is like a beautiful woman: a pleasure for the whole body."

The lieutenant furrowed his brow and gave a threatening look, but then, remembering that he wasn't in the square house, he forced a smile.

Awa brought hot water, soap, and a towel. On her knees, she presented the bucket before each guest, waiting for each to finish washing his hands. Then she offered each a small toothpick and a large white kola nut.

"It is an honor to my household," she said to the lieutenant, "that the steps that led you to me were those of friendship."

"For a path not to be swallowed by the grass, it must be traveled regularly," replied the lieutenant, stressing each word.

The conversation stretched late into the night.

The lieutenant exulted:

"The hat! Well, I haven't tried it, but I feel that it's my size. I like her figure, her color. If Awa ordered me to step into the fire, I would hurry on in. Of course, I'd come out running."

"This time, Lieutenant, you need to move fast," Fadiala suggested.

"Speak clearly and to the point," said the lieutenant.

"To speak clearly would be to speak frankly, and I know that you're short-tempered."

"You're thinking about those penniless young men who pay court to Awa, who wear such tight pants that they have to coat their thighs with oil? How could a woman like Awa be attracted to such characters?"

"Lieutenant, you must catch the june bug while he's cold."

"Agreed."

"Confide your interests to a local mediator to prepare for marriage."

. . .

The next day, the lieutenant sent for Solo, an old blind man. It was said that his speech could put out a fire, and that he needed only a few well-chosen words to start a quarrel. When Kouta's elders met, old Solo sat outside the circle and, without appearing to listen, drank up the words of each man. Then, asking to speak: "Blind, I know neither fear nor shame." Thus he would support one argument, slicing up another with his knife-sharp tongue. And once he'd separated the wheat from the chaff, no one knew what else to say.

Many stories about him made the rounds. One day, the governor-general of all of the West African colonies came to Kouta, hoping to carry back a large quantity of *kinkéliba*[2] leaves, known for their medicinal properties. Distracted by the ceremony and by the many beautiful women he was honoring, he had forgotten to make the request to Commandant Dotori. Arriving in Darako, he sent an urgent telegram saying that he wished to receive one ton of *kinkéliba* leaves by the next morning's five o'clock train. The telegram arrived late at night. The panicked commandant summoned all the elders to his home.

"There goes my promotion, and maybe my rank," he complained.

"So what's the problem?" Old Solo asked.

"A ton of *kinkéliba* to be picked in one night; that's a lot!"

"No, Commandant!" Solo replied. "Open the prison doors, and order the inmates to search the hills. Of course, only some will survive; others will be bitten by nasty snakes . . ."

The commandant shook Solo's hand. From that day forward, Solo became his friend and informant.

Commandant Bertin had succeeded Dotori, who was given early retirement; it was said that he'd become too familiar with the natives.

"Bertin is madder than a donkey with its dick cut off," the people said. One day, he ordered the town crier to warn the people that those who didn't pay their taxes before the end of the week would face the traditional torture: an iron ring placed upon a clean-shaven head, and a large rock placed atop the ring.

While everyone thrashed about, some running to take out new loans from merchants and ex-soldiers, others reclaiming old debts, Solo, in broad daylight, lit a kerosene lamp and came down the village's main road. The cercle guards, more scared than surprised, reported the incident to the clerks, and the clerks reported it to the commandant. Solo was sent for, and he explained.

"It's my way of looking for taxes," he said.

Commandant Bertin laughed until he cried, and then wrote in the register in his own hand: "exempted from taxes forever."

The people of Kouta considered Solo clever, though not all meant it to his credit.

"He does business with one hand above the table and the other beneath," they said.

"People of Kouta," he explained, "don't ask me to shell the peanuts if you don't want me to munch on a few."

They held against him a trick that he'd played upon Daouda, a rich merchant. Solo had acted as an intermediary between Daouda and the family of a young divorcée; as usual, he conducted the business successfully. The day of the wedding and the amount of the dowry were then agreed upon. Daouda claimed he had given the money to Solo, but Solo claimed the opposite. The disagreement reached the ears of Commandant Bertin.

"Work this business out like natives," he concluded.

The elders recommended that the two take a vow on the Koran after the Friday prayer.

"Then you want to sully God's word with some argument over a woman?" Solo threatened.

The imam agreed.

"In the whole history of Kouta, there has never been such a vow, and as long as I'm your imam, there will not be."

Daouda complained to the chief of the canton. One Thursday, the chief called together the two parties and all of the elders except the imam.

"Kouta relies on a fetish that pardons neither treachery nor infamy," he said. "Let Daouda and Solo swear solemnly upon this fetish."

Solo refused.

"Then you confirm the accusations?" asked the chief.

"No!"

"I don't understand."

Solo took a moment to order his thoughts and find the thread of his argument:

"When a bastard and a man of noble birth swear upon a fetish, it turns away from the bastard to attack the man whose mother and father are known."

Daouda's whole body started to shake, and he left the gathering, his eyes bloodshot. And from that day forward, the villagers of Kouta doubted the honesty of Daouda's origins.

■　　■　　■

The lieutenant explained his plan to Solo, sparing no detail. He felt the joy of a young man, attributing to Awa every quality one could wish for in a wife.

"You see, I want to marry her as soon as possible."

Solo remained impassive, his dead eyes fixed on the lieutenant.

"In truth," he finally said, "Awa is a beautiful woman. Teeth made to shine in the sun, skin so black you could see your reflection. You know, Lieutenant, black is beautiful."

"A blind man praising a woman's looks?" the lieutenant asked, amazed.

"Of course! I see her with my mind; I see her through the eyes of others by what people say about her."

"Don't you dare trick me!" the lieutenant shouted. "If you get it in your head to betray my trust, I'll put you down with my revolver, like a dog."

"I know you're capable of it," Solo replied calmly.

"And the commandant . . ."

"He wouldn't even send for you. No white commandant would imprison an ex-soldier for the murder of an old blind man exempted from his taxes." Solo took on a sad, almost compassionate look and added, "This marriage will be difficult, perhaps impossible."

"What did you just say?" the lieutenant roared.

"You heard me fine," Solo said, his finger pointed as if pronouncing a court sentence.

"Impossible?"

"There's already someone in place, and he knows his way around women."

The lieutenant leapt up, his trembling hands catching Solo's boubou.

"Who? Tell me, who?" He let go, baffled. "Awa received me so kindly."

"A man who pays for a meal is always well received. The people of Kouta have had a lot to say about that dinner."

The lieutenant didn't want to know more and went back on the attack.

"You spoke of someone—what's his name? Tell me his name!"

"Never, Lieutenant. Contrary to rumor, I'm a man who keeps my promises."

"They say you're corrupt! And that you take advantage of the girls yourself before passing on the marriage offers!"

"Corrupt! All poor people are, and they stop only when they escape their misery. Then they buy the approval of those who are still poor. Me, take advantage of the girls? It's slander. A blind man would be insane to slander like that. At least I don't have that problem."

"How much did you get from my rival?"

"Enough to not betray him."

Solo did a mental calculation, checked it and rechecked it, counting on the lieutenant's desperation.

"One goes to hell to escape the cold. My price is three thousand francs."

"Too expensive for me."

Solo pretended to get up.

"Wait," said the lieutenant, pulling out his wallet.

"That's the right amount," the old man snickered. "I recognize the thousand franc notes by their scent; they smell of the perfume that the rich wear. These notes here have only passed through the hands of the poor."

"Now, who?" the lieutenant demanded.

"Soriba," Solo blurted, as if exhausted.

"That libertine! That cad!"

"You must always evaluate your rival calmly. Insults are an admission of weakness."

"But he already has three wives, and he's as scraggly as a tree on its last root."

"Old Soriba wants Awa for a fourth wife to make his leaves green again. And if he were to marry her, his white temples would go back to gray. You don't know, Lieutenant, just how much a woman can change a man. It's like a good diet."

"Obviously, you'll explain to him that I'm already in and that he must withdraw."

"I know Old Soriba well enough to tell you that doing that would be a grave mistake. When it comes to women, he's more stubborn than a donkey. Instead, I'll discredit him with Awa by tarnishing his reputation."

"Don't you dare trick me, Solo!" He furrowed his brow and forced a smile. "If you trick me . . ."

"I know, you'll kill me with a revolver. And the commandant will say: 'that's fine.'" Solo started to laugh without restraint, as if taunting the lieutenant.

"You know, in the village, people think your rifle shots are only the sound of gunpowder. I can't disagree. The Whites are busy massacring each other again, and they're not sending any bullets out this way."

8.

FAMAKAN HAD COME HOME FROM SCHOOL IN TEARS. HE THREW HIS SCHOOL bag on the table and rushed into the lieutenant's arms.

"What happened, little man?"

Famakan didn't answer and began crying even harder.

"Come on, they made one of your favorite foods today: fonio with peanut sauce."

The child refused to listen; he broke free of the lieutenant's embrace and went to shut himself in his room. His father followed him there and, without saying a word, sat on the edge of the bed, next to his weeping son. The lieutenant felt his anger rising, but kept control.

"You broke our pact, little man. We promised not to keep secrets from each other."

He tried evoking the past in hope of seeing a smile on his son's lips.

"Famakan, this egg—was it you who laid it?"

Usually this joke cheered him up. The boy would laugh his head off, and all the square house laughed with him.

"Maybe you've seen a shirt that you like? Well then, I'll buy it for you."

The child shook his head.

"Did an older boy hit you? What's his name? Tell me his name, and I promise he'll regret it."

"No," Famakan said. "Nobody hits me anymore, not even the teacher."

The lieutenant left the room, tortured by dark thoughts.

"Perhaps he's distressed over my marriage announcement. He thinks that he won't get enough attention."

He shouted from under the shade hangar outside:

"Since you refuse to eat, well then no one will swallow a single bite. I'm punishing everybody, including myself."

Then the child came to him, head bowed, and sat on his knees.

"Somebody insulted my father," he said, indignant.

"And what did he say?" the lieutenant snickered.

"He named the parts of my father."

"I promise, Famakan, that such insults will not make you cry again," the lieutenant vowed, a spark of malice in his eyes.

■ ■ ■

The teacher was circulating among the students, threatening some with his cane, stroking the heads of others, when the lieutenant arrived at the school. The boys and girls rose from their seats.

"Hello, Lieutenant."

"Hello, children."

The teacher didn't hide his surprise and noticed that Siriman Keita returned his greetings coldly.

"I'll get right to the point," the lieutenant said. "One of your students insulted me and left my son in a very worrying state of nerves." And turning to Famakan: "Show him to me!"

The child pointed out one of his classmates. The lieutenant beckoned for the boy to approach.

"Go tell your father that the teacher asked him to come."

"You know that insults are the first words that children learn," the teacher said. "What can you do?"

"Go tell your father to come," the lieutenant roared.

The little boy set off running and came back right away, proudly holding his father's hand.

While everyone was expecting a physical punishment, Siriman Keita dropped his pants, turned around, spread his legs, and leaned forward against the blackboard.

For more than five minutes, he exposed his *kotafla*,[3] which shone like well-polished leather. Then he rebuttoned his fly and grabbed the other child's father.

"Now, it's your turn to show us the king's two counselors."

■   ■   ■

"That, Lieutenant," Solo complained, "makes my job very difficult. Doing that, and a week before your wedding! Naturally, it's the talk of the village."

"And what are they saying?"

"That you took off your pants in class, and forced this poor Diango to do the same. Your enemies exaggerated the incident. They told the whole village you'd do it again in the middle of the marketplace. Awa was on the verge of withdrawing her consent. Of course, I spun a story that I planted here and there. I started the rumor that it was a visual aid for a lesson. And the young teacher confirmed my story in exchange for my silence."

"Your silence?" the stunned lieutenant asked.

"Well yes! He knocked up a fifteen-year-old girl."

"And how much do I owe you?"

"Save me from the butcher. He's the only one I'm afraid of. I haven't been allowed in the butcher's shop for a week!"

"You, afraid of someone?"

"More than anything in the world, I love meat. And Namori the butcher never forgets a debt, nor tires of reclaiming it."

9.

THE LIEUTENANT DEMANDED A MARRIAGE WITHOUT RELIGIOUS CEREMONY. His humiliation at the hands of the imam still stung whenever he thought of it. And what would Faganda have said if he knew that his brother had been made a fool of in front of the marabouts? He would surely have spoken of treason.

"I've decided to get married in front of the commandant," the lieutenant said to Solo.

"A civil marriage?" the old man exclaimed. "Kouta's never had one before."

"It's faster! Instead of saying 'I shaved my head,' it's easier to just take off your hat."

"A civil marriage is sometimes very expensive; when you want to divorce, it takes discussions and negotiations, reconciliations and separations, lawyers and judges. Think about it some more, Lieutenant."

"My decision is irrevocable. I want a civil marriage. Somebody has to set the example. It's a guarantee for women."

Commandant Bertin agreed to act as the lieutenant's witness and designated a clerk to act as Awa's.

That very evening, she moved into the square house, veiled in white, escorted by several older women who half-heartedly sang a bridal song:

Your father's house
was pleasant, Awa Konaté!
But everything pleasant
has an end, Awa Konaté!

Though traditional and dating back to the beginning of time, this song displeased the lieutenant. He dismissed the women, giving them a thousand francs, and ordered his courtiers to deal with his wife's luggage: trunks, kitchen utensils, everything that a young wife brings to her marital home. Two of her cousins sat on the threshold.

"She will not enter until her husband has paid her fee."

Siriman Keita generously offered them five hundred francs.

Solo gave the newlyweds the usual advice and then spoke directly to the lieutenant.

"Siriman," he said, "here is Awa, your wife. I have brought her to you intact. She is neither one-eyed nor one-legged, and she is missing no teeth. Her milk teeth have fallen, replaced long ago by teeth that shine like the sun."

It was the first time that Solo had called him by his first name, like a father.

"People say I'm violent, but I know to respect beautiful things."

"Siriman," Solo continued, "you must only insult a woman if she has done something that merits a beating, and you must only beat her for a fault that, in all justice, requires death."

The courtiers approved of this wise advice.

"Scold the cat and warn the mouse," Solo affirmed. He turned to Awa. "Here is Siriman, your husband. He's a thief. Say: 'he's a thief!'"

"He's a thief."

"He's a skirt chaser. Say: 'he's a skirt chaser!'"

"He's a skirt chaser."

The courtiers and the lieutenant started to laugh and slap their thighs.

"You see, my girl, Kouta suffers from a great evil: slander. The elders have yet to find a remedy, because they're the ones responsible for it. As they say, a man can't find a needle he's hiding under his own foot. Every time they tell you Siriman's a thief or a skirt chaser, say that you knew that before marrying him."

The wedding night was about to begin. The lieutenant went into the enclosure that served as a shower and latrine. A bucket of hot water awaited him; he took his nuptial bath. On his way out, Solo stopped him.

"Did you remember the rooster?"

"The rooster? For what?"

"You're so clueless! Slit its throat and spread a little blood on the sheets."

"Awa and I consummated our relationship on our third evening together."

"Everybody knows that, but it's tradition. And don't break it. Women, especially those who no longer receive their husbands' honors, love to see a nuptial sheet spotted with blood; and for the impotent men, it reminds them of their past virility. Certain elders—I won't say their names—have confided in me that at the sight of a nuptial sheet, their desire, which they thought long extinguished, reawakens."

The lieutenant burst into side-splitting laughter.

"No!" he said, one hand over his lips to try to contain himself.

"Well, if you insist, I'll have to take you into my confidence: the imam—yes, I said the imam . . ."

"No!" the lieutenant cried, his eyes bulging.

"While waiting for the houris promised by the Prophet, for more than ten years, his only pleasure in this world has been to see a nuptial sheet. You don't know the village that you live in. In Kouta, the hyena's mother was both buried and dug up in the presence of the vulture."

"Who's the hyena?"

"All those who live in Kouta. And the vulture, that's me."

Little by little, their laughter ceased. Solo dug a hand into the pocket of his boubou and took out a vial of kola nut paste infused with salt, ground *sinsan*[4] root, and a bit of red pepper.

"Take this," he said, holding it out to the lieutenant. "Eat it. It doesn't taste very good. Eat all of it, and wait a moment for it to take effect. Tonight, Lieutenant, you must perform."

"I've never had any problem with that."

"You never know. With all the emotion, I've seen young people who can normally keep a girl up all week long go soft and limp on their wedding nights. Then the relatives took back their daughter, and the dowry, the clothing, and the matchmaker's salary all had to be returned. Be prudent, Lieutenant. Close your eyes and eat it."

Solo left after giving his best wishes and blessings, promising to come at the first light of dawn with the procession of women who would carry the nuptial sheet through the village.

The lieutenant found a light-skinned girl with a large rump in his bed, smiling at him.

"You'll pay Awa's friends for the *primae noctis*, or you'll deflower me in her place. And tomorrow morning, I'll give you such a reputation that people will flee from you like a mangy dog."

Siriman Keita gave a thousand francs; the young girl got up, and Awa appeared, uncovering her face.

∎   ∎   ∎

The lieutenant woke up early, his eyes dull, his mouth pasty. His head spun and his stomach rumbled. His gaze lingered on Awa, asleep beneath the mosquito net, broken, conquered, offered up to him. Her pagne was untied and exposed half of a breast gleaming with sweat, rising and falling to the rhythm of her breathing.

"That crook Solo is right," he said to himself. "Black is beautiful."

A shiver seized him; he mastered it and stretched out, yawning and cracking his joints. He took a hot bath and relieved himself to calm the burning of his stomach.

"The rooster! I forgot the rooster," he said.

Before slitting its throat, the lieutenant strangled it so that it wouldn't crow.

"Now it's time to stretch my legs a bit," he told himself with a sigh of satisfaction.

Outside the gate, he met Solo, who came for news, escorted by several women.

"Lieutenant, how did everything go?" he asked. He seemed worried.

"Murderer!" the lieutenant exploded. "You almost killed me with your poisons. I'm having heart palpitations."

"I came for the rooster. Did you slit its throat?"

"Just now, and I stained the sheet with blood."

"How did you do it?"

"Well, I spread some blood under Awa's thighs."

Solo started to laugh.

"That, Lieutenant, is a flood. Nobody will believe that's from a deflowering. Do you have another sheet?"

"No!" the lieutenant said angrily. His stomach was burning, and he needed to relieve himself again.

Solo turned to one of the women.

"Doussouba, cut the nuptial sheet in two; plunge your finger into the blood and place it on the sheet three times in a straight line."

"Dirty old man! Who taught you all that?"

"You, Doussouba. And if Awa had made love to another before her marriage, it's you I would have asked to sew her a second virginity. I have never figured out how you do that."

The woman grew angry, straightened her emaciated body to its full height, and hurled insults at Solo's father, his mother, and all those who had preceded him in his line.

"Such insults, and on such a beautiful morning!" the old man snickered. "The whole neighborhood will hear you."

The lieutenant ran to relieve himself and then came back, holding his stomach.

"I almost forgot," said the old man. "Nobody in your household should eat this rooster, or else your marriage will be unhappy."

"Take it, you swindler! Murderer!"

Solo held out the rooster to Doussouba, who smiled broadly, sliding it into a calabash beneath the nuptial sheet.

A donkey started to bray in the courtyard. The lieutenant rushed over and was seized with fear when he took in the full spectacle: a donkey! A donkey with both ears cut off, the wounds still bleeding! He went back to Solo to tell him what he had seen.

"An enemy wants to take your life; someone wants you to go away to the land of the white bones. But don't worry; you can cut iron with iron. It's thought that transforms millet into wine. Give me some time to reflect."

The women paraded the nuptial sheet all through the village, from house to house, dancing to the cheerful sound of the talking drum. The women who were excused from their domestic duties that morning joined them, and soon there was a party in the village square. The older women, their lips red with kola juice, went around the circle, gesturing symbolically. When they finished their march, the young girls took over. They stomped their feet to a rhythm that started slow, then became faster and faster, their movements becoming gradually choppier. Soon their shoulders and breasts shook with frenzied jolts; they finished in contortions so intense that fat drops of sweat ran down their bare chests. After a short break, which the drummers used to warm their instruments, a clear, loud voice pronounced the chorus of a song, which was taken up by all the participants. This was the tribute to Awa's virginity.

The dance began again, and the enthusiasm knew no limits. The joy became delirious. And Solo, presiding over the party, moved into the middle of the circle, his raised arms demanding silence.

"Awa is an honest woman," he said. "Her husband found her in her home. Her nuptial sheet proves it. And to honor her, Lieutenant Siriman Keita offers her fifty grams of gold."

The crowd applauded frantically.

"He also ordered me to distribute two thousand francs to pay for kola nuts for all those who participated in his joy."

The square emptied, everybody happy, while the drummers played muted rolls with the tips of their fingers.

■　　■　　■

That evening, Solo came to the square house accompanied by a witch doctor of great renown.

"Siriman, this is N'Pé. He is so loaded with knowledge that he can stop the rain from falling on a day of celebration. To send somebody into another world, he need only crush a sorghum seed with his hammer. But he is not God. A human being exists only in small part above the earth; much of him is beneath. Those who give death die themselves."

"Death herself will die one day," N'Pé declared.

The lieutenant explained his agony. N'Pé gave him stealthy glances without ever looking him in the eye. Every now and then, the witch doctor asked an insignificant question, noted the response, and asked the same question again in a different, more precise way. When he had determined the problem in its entirety, he stared at the lieutenant for a while, forcing him to lower his eyes.

N'Pé struck vertical lines into the sand and then erased them.

"Adama, mute!" he said. "Nuhun is also silent. And Ba-Awa is sterile."

He took a flask from his bag, washed his face, and wet the sand. He made horizontal lines in groups of three and seven and carefully examined them, his forehead creased. The lieutenant's heart beat heavily. His gaze passed endlessly between the sand and the witch doctor's tense face.

"Iblissa⁵ has come down!" N'Pé shouted. "He can always be chased away; he is not God."

He erased the signs, redrew some vertical lines cutting a horizontal one, and announced:

"Siriman Keita, this donkey must not die! No, it must not. The sand says that the donkey that yields offspring will chase the misfortune from your house and return it to him who wished it upon you. Siriman Keita, the sand says that the poorly constructed well collapses upon what? Upon itself! Now Adama speaks, and Nuhun echoes. And what do they say? That no enemy may triumph against you."

He gathered the sand into a pile and put it back into his bag.

"I am only an interpreter, and if I have lied, the spirits must have wished it."

The lieutenant rose and paid generously.

10.

THE LIEUTENANT DAWDLED AROUND THE CLINIC FOR SOME TIME WITHOUT making up his mind to go in. You go tell a French doctor that somebody sent you a fetish donkey, and if it dies, the ancestors will take you by the hand . . . Several passersby stopped to compliment him on his marriage, the lovely gift he had given Awa, and the beautiful celebration with which he had honored the village. He barely forced a smile, almost grimacing, in response to each. And when the congratulations went on too long, he cut them short, claiming an urgent errand.

A crafty idea came to him, and he hurried into the clinic to make use of it, going straight to the nurse who was dressing wounds.

"My son Famakan is a funny boy, always restless and energetic, and he often comes home covered in scrapes. Could you give me a little Mercurochrome? I'll take care of him myself."

The nurse didn't deign to lift his eyes and administered a resounding slap to the patient he was treating.

"You have to hold your leg straight for the bandage to stick. Patients are rotten as carrion and don't follow the advice that they're given. Tomorrow I'll put some iodine and healing agent on your wound. Let me tell you, they'll hear you bawling for miles! Next!"

Another patient climbed onto the table with the help of a cane. N'Godé sprinkled his wound with a scorching permanganate solution, ripped off the bandage with his tweezers, and threw it in the wastebasket, turning his head: "Not even a hyena would want this one."

Finally he raised his eyes to Siriman Keita.

"What were you saying, Lieutenant?"

"N'Godé, I'd like a little Mercurochrome. My son . . ."

"You didn't answer my question."

"Perhaps I'll understand better outside?"

N'Godé threw his tweezers onto a tray, wiped his hands with alcohol, and left with the lieutenant.

"Here's enough for a kola nut," Siriman Keita said, holding out a hundred franc note.

"Well said, Lieutenant. That's how a man speaks!"

He cleaned out an old vial, filled it with Mercurochrome, and handed it to the lieutenant.

"Whenever you need more, you can send somebody to me, or ask me to deliver it to your house."

"A little hydrocolloid might be handy."

N'Godé filled a cone with powder and, as a show of good faith, also offered the lieutenant some bandages.

■   ■   ■

For a week, the lieutenant, barely awake, devoted himself to the donkey's care. He cleaned its ears with eau de cologne, smeared them in Mercurochrome, and covered them in sulfa drugs. The wounds still festered. The donkey was wasting away despite all of the care being lavished on it. One courtier had to bring it a bucket of water three times a day. Another was ordered to supply it with sorghum. Yet still the lieutenant's donkey was losing weight.

One morning, Siriman awoke to see the donkey collapsed on its side, breathing deeply and covered by a swarm of flies.

His legs giving way, his whole body trembling, he went to the clinic, telling himself, "If you say the world's a good place to live, it's because you have both feet in it. Let them mock me as much as they want, so long as I'm alive. The dead no longer hear such taunts."

Leroy, the French doctor, greeted him with a joke: "It seems, Lieutenant, that the beautiful Awa already has you a bit tired. You'll see, there's a rhythm to pick up."

"It's not that, Colonel," the lieutenant said, not knowing how to explain his problem.

"I'm a military doctor—we could have served in the same company. So speak frankly."

He dismissed the patient whose breathing he was checking.

"Pulmonary tuberculosis! It's a scourge in this country. And they come to me only after they've tried every traditional remedy, in vain. Some have real curative powers, I don't deny it. But Western medicine has been proven. You understand, I'm no racist. I'm writing an official report. You have a big role to play among others of your race. In less than a month, that one'll be dead. And what do you want me to do about it? Too late—it's too late."

He got up, rubbed his hands energetically with alcohol, and lit a cigarette.

"I'm listening, Lieutenant."

"My brother just sent me a donkey that's giving me a lot of trouble."

"Ah!" the doctor exclaimed.

"Because it was refusing to cooperate, my brother, who's bad-tempered, cut off its ears. I've tried everything—Mercurochrome, sulfa drugs—but nothing does the trick."

"Did you see the veterinarian?"

The lieutenant's face darkened. He was struggling to think up a lie when Leroy exclaimed:

"How silly of me! He's been on his rounds for a whole month now. Here's what I can do. It's unusual. You understand that the clinic suffers from a shortage of medicine. Every morning, for a week, I'll send a nurse to give your donkey a shot of penicillin. And believe me, I'm doing this just for you."

The lieutenant arrived at Old Soriba's house around noon.

He found the man seated under the shade hangar in front of his house, shirtless, a brightly colored pagne around his waist. A large plate rested on the ground before him, around which his wives busied themselves. One was mixing the sauce with the rice, the second was deboning the fish, and the last, with the help of a fan, was cooling the master of the house.

Soriba took big handfuls, choking, coughing, clearing his throat noisily. When he stopped eating, it was to ask for water.

"There's a man who's covered with women," the lieutenant said to himself, feeling a twinge of jealousy.

To his greeting, Soriba replied, "Are the steps that brought you to my house those of friendship?"

"Friendship only," said the lieutenant. "The feet do not go where the heart is not."

"It's the truth!" Soriba agreed. "So, friend, share my meal."

"It's just that I've already eaten."

"Ah! He who doesn't honor my wives' cooking, Lieutenant, is no friend of mine."

Siriman Keita washed his hands in some grayish water, squatted down, and took several pieces of fish, which he swallowed without chewing.

"I've satisfied the custom."

Old Soriba had not finished eating. Once the plate was empty, he would give a look and be resupplied. From time to time, he would swallow a big cup of water in one gulp, sigh with satisfaction, and sneeze. One of his wives would slap him on the back, and then he would go back to eating.

The lieutenant was boiling with impatience. When his gaze crossed Soriba's, he would smile to mask his astonishment and indignation. Suddenly, a burp resounded. Old Soriba blessed his meal by reciting the profession of faith. He licked his fingers thoroughly, one finger after another, and then soaked them in the bucket of water, before wiping them off on his hair.

"Lieutenant, I like direct and concise conversations."

"I'm told you raise donkeys."

"That's true. I have a soft spot for donkeys; I got it from my father, who was also fond of them. Each time that they heard '*kourou nama*,' the people of Kouta cried, 'It's old Drissa returning with his donkeys.'"

"I'm going to speak frankly, though I say this in complete confidence. Someone who wishes me harm for some fuss over a woman has just sent me a fetish donkey with the ears cut off."

"Think of that! How awful people are!"

"Oh, I put him back on his feet; he's out of danger. It's just that he's a little bored, and I thought that he'd be happier if I found him a lady friend."

Old Soriba looked at Siriman Keita, a triumphant smile on his lips.

"That's a problem," he said. "I only set one jenny aside for breeding. And if I were to sell her, my donkeys would be bored. But an arrangement is always possible."

"What arrangement?" the lieutenant whispered.

"If you bought my whole herd?"

The lieutenant opened his eyes wide with astonishment, and Soriba saw that he was trembling with anguish.

"I thought that you were going to lend me your jenny, and when a foal was born, I would have bought it . . ."

"Then the jenny, when it returned, would carry your misfortune into my house."

He stared at the lieutenant, laughing inwardly at his discomfort. The muezzin gave the call to prayer.

"It's Friday, the day of the great prayer, and I still haven't done my ablutions. I wish you good day, Lieutenant. I see we're not going to come to an agreement."

"Let's at least discuss the price."

"Let's see," Old Soriba replied, "five jackasses and one jenny, what's that worth nowadays? Five jackasses and one jenny, all of them grain-fed. Of course, I always move too fast when it comes to business. My father used to reproach me for it: 'Soriba, you never take time to reflect before making a deal. At that price, you'll never make your fortune.' That's what my late father would say. I almost forgot the caretaker's pay."

He began a meticulous, interminable mental calculation, counting on his fingers.

"No!" he said.

He did it again, muttering. Then, in a loud voice:

"Twenty thousand francs, and no bargaining! I'm in a hurry. The imam has never beaten me to the mosque."

"Have them brought to the square house. I'll send you the money."

Soriba had stood up. He glared at the lieutenant, impressing the man with his self-assurance.

"The money!" he said. "Money likes to be counted when it passes from one hand to another, without a go-between."

"In that case, I'll come back after the prayer."

Immediately after the lieutenant had come to collect his donkeys and pay Old Soriba hand to hand, with neither go-between nor witness, Solo appeared at the latter's shade hangar.

"The crocodile's meat is succulent," he said, "but when it cools, it gets sticky. I've come for my share."

"Speaking of meat," Old Soriba replied, "there's a plate under the *tara*.[6] You can tell me the latest news."

"I'm poor but proud!" Solo shot back. "I don't live off of other people's leftovers."

"Who said anything about leftovers?" Old Soriba countered. "You always have to bicker with me, ever since we were circumcised together. You always have to see bad intentions in everyone."

"You ate before going to the mosque. The leftovers are supposed to be given to the needy. To keep them is a sign of selfishness! Of wickedness! It's a profane act; it's *jahiliya*!"[7]

"Well, to say that 'I ate' . . ."

"Did you eat? Yes or no?" Solo shouted.

"I moved my lips . . ."

"Because you weren't hungry. So therefore it's your leftovers that you're offering me. I don't want them! Eating leftovers is my family's taboo."

Old Soriba called one of his wives and asked her to bring a bucket of water.

"What are you doing?" Solo asked.

"Eating! Eating my leftovers."

"Well then, for me, they're no longer leftovers; leftovers are when the man of the house is satisfied and has pushed away the plate."

They washed their hands. Old Soriba put some sauce on the fonio and kept all of the pieces of meat in reach. He took his first handful and put it on the plate, scratching his side noisily.

"You know, Solo," he said, "you're my brother by circumcision, my more-than-brother. We were circumcised on the same day and with the same knife. And I've often broken certain customs to please you."

"I see how it is!" Solo thundered. "A man can be wrong about a plate of fonio set aside for him, but never the malicious words addressed to him."

He set down the handful that he was about to eat.

"You don't want to eat with a blind man. Is that really it?"

"You're my brother by circumcision . . ."

"But a blind brother by circumcision. And you'd like me to eat out of a separate dish."

"It's the custom; there's nothing I can do about it."

"Well then, so be it! The dog doesn't eat with his master."

Old Soriba divided the fonio into two almost-equal portions and put two pieces of meat on Solo's share. The two men started eating.

"This is really well done!" Solo exclaimed after his third mouthful. "I'd bet this fonio was made by your first wife."

"What makes you say that?"

"This fonio's well done, I tell you. It was left in water overnight to soften. And instead of cooking it as inexperienced women do, this has been steamed. And to ease its trip, a pinch of ground baobab leaves was added. As for the sauce . . . the peanut leaves were boiled to extract that slightly bitter taste they have. And as for the meat . . ."

Old Soriba had no desire to hear the rest.

"Amy!" he called. "Solo has complimented you greatly for this fonio with peanut leaves. Everyone in Kouta knows that Solo and Soriba are as different as milk and lemon. Well, for once we agree. It's real cooking—cooking done without haste!"

"Tactless!" Solo said. "From now on, you'll have your other two wives against you. It's like you just offered your first wife new clothes with the other two right here watching."

Old Soriba turned so that his voice carried through the compound. "God of Heaven, venerated be your Prophet! You have given me three wives, and I don't know whose cooking is best."

The men ate in silence, while the women, giddy with Old Soriba's compliments, went laughing from room to room.

"I like eating in joy," Solo said. "This plate of fonio is a call to joy."

Old Soriba laughed without really understanding the allusion.

"The joy of a moment," he said, nostalgic. "The stomach is so ungrateful! You feed it so well, yet a few hours later . . ."

"This fonio is a call to joy, I'm telling you. It has aphrodisiacs in it."

"Aphrodisiacs! How do you know? Aphrodisiacs!"

"By this flavor of incense, which camouflages the taste."

"Aphrodisiacs," Old Soriba said again.

"All women put them in their husbands' food," Solo said casually.

"And how are they made?"

"No, Soriba! I don't want to talk about that while I'm eating. Nogobri would be better able to tell you. He's the supplier for all the women in the village."

"But surely you have some idea, Solo?" He breathed deeply, his arms dangling, his nostrils trembling. "Incense," he said, "fragrance of paradise . . ."

"Yes, incense," replied Solo. "That's the pleasant side of aphrodisiacs. It's the packaging."

"And the contents?"

"Stop pinching my ribs with your questions," Solo said impatiently. "Go see Nogobri."

"So to find out, I have to go ask a stranger, even though my circumcision brother could save me the trip . . ."

"Fine," Solo spat. "You asked for it. Well, aphrodisiacs . . ."

He stopped, rolled an enormous handful of fonio, and chewed it at length.

"Aphrodisiacs, they contain just about everything imaginable, particularly the genitals of animals known for their ruts. Nogobri told me that the dog and the monkey . . ."

He paused for a moment and took a piece of meat.

"Let's leave it at that," he murmured. "This evening your first wife calls you to joy, drawing you from afar like a moth."

Old Soriba put down his handful and pushed away the plate.

"I don't feel very well anymore. An itch is tickling my guts, and it's climbing toward my stomach."

"Already?" Solo asked, astonished. "Should I leave? But tomorrow morning, I beg you, tell me all about it."

"I want to vomit," Old Soriba said.

"I know an excellent remedy: rub your forefinger in your armpit and then put it up to your nose."

Old Soriba did as Solo suggested and then pushed the plate across. "You can eat my share," he said.

"Your leftovers! Never!"

"They're not leftovers. I'm still hungry, Solo. Before going to the mosque, I take a few handfuls and one or two pieces of meat. It's when I get back that I really eat."

"The meat? I won't say no. And stop telling me you need to vomit. Just get it over with, and let's stop talking about it."

Old Soriba left the shade hangar and returned a little while later, his mouth dripping with saliva.

"Women," he said, "whether they love or hate . . . Aphrodisiacs in my food?

My father would tell me: 'Soriba, love your wife, but be as vigilant with her as with a river that floods.' I'm about to throw up."

"I know another remedy for vomiting, and if that proves ineffective, you'll have to consult a doctor. Think hard; deduce one idea from another. For example, tell me this: why do you send your children to the school of the Whites?"

"Because manual labor doesn't pay. A clerk makes ten times more than a laborer."

"And does that seem fair to you?"

"Absolutely! School is expensive, and education takes time. To educate yourself is to throw away money to get it back later. And that's not all. Not everybody can be educated. You have to be intelligent. In fact, the clerk is better paid than the laborer because he's intelligent."

"So in other words, an intelligent man should be better paid than somebody who's not."

"Giving money to an idiot is, as they say, like asking a Moor, a man of the desert, to manage the field work from clearing to harvesting. And it never rains in the desert. Lieutenant Siriman Keita, for example . . ."

"Speaking of which, Soriba, the donkeys were sold at a usurious price, thanks to my efforts . . ."

"They were my donkeys, and I lost one in the operation."

"Lost a donkey?" Solo protested. "He was so skinny that Namori the butcher wouldn't take him. He told you he couldn't mix that meat in with the beef."

Old Soriba ripped a straw from a mat and picked at his teeth. He took the cup and filled his mouth with water. His cheeks swelled and sagged like the bellows of a forge. He took a long rinse and spat.

"I despise you, Solo!" he shouted. "I cast you out forever, and like this spilled water, you are permanently expelled from my company."

Silence set in, dry and oppressive. Old Soriba took Solo by the shoulder and thumped him on the back.

"I let my anger get the best of me," he said by way of excuse. "A man cut by the same knife can never be cast out."

"Never," Solo agreed.

"So let's split the money equally, as we did the plate of fonio."

Solo took a kola nut from his pocket, split it in two, and offered half to Old Soriba.

"You understand, Soriba," he complained, "our parts can't be equal. I've sinned too much in this business. Cutting off a donkey's ears—who else would have accepted such a task? To bribe a witch doctor is to make friends with the devil. And I will pay all of these debts when I appear before God. Soriba, our shares can't be equal. I must get five thousand francs more than you."

Old Soriba took out the bundle of notes and counted them slowly between his saliva-coated forefinger and thumb.

"Well, if the dispute hinges on five thousand francs, let's split the difference. That way we save our brotherhood, and I shoulder much of your sin."

Solo counted his money, taking his time.

"I don't like your math," he said. "I have here, between my fingers, nine notes of a thousand francs and one note of five hundred, instead of twelve notes of a thousand and one of five hundred."

"Yes," Old Soriba said nonchalantly. "I took out the three thousand francs that I gave you when I was angling for Awa's hand."

"I don't like your math," Solo repeated.

They both laughed and shared a second kola nut.

"With this business," Old Soriba said, "I've added just enough to my capital to open a shop."

"Tell me your plans," Solo exclaimed. "I'll give you such publicity that Daouda will burst with jealousy."

"Daouda and I have come to an understanding. While he sells plain-weave fabric, I'll sell patterned fabric. A millet shortage at Daouda's store will send everybody to buy it at Soriba's."

"And Soriba will raise the price, to set fire to the anuses of the poor people of Kouta."

"When there's no rice in Soriba's store, they'll have to go to Daouda's."

"That guy, as I know him . . ." Solo stopped, ready to tear his hair with rage. "If money was covered in shit and thrown in the fire, Daouda would go chasing it. He'll double the price for sure."

"And to encourage people to buy, there'll be a good publicist, a drum that sounds without needing to be struck. And this drum . . ."

"Solo! The dog who is satisfied with crumbs! Well, for once, Soriba, I say no!"

He took his leave, saying to himself: "Daouda is going to open a second shop—and Soriba is the manager."

. . .

In Kouta, they no longer said "the square house" when referring to the lieutenant's residence. The villagers had nicknamed it "the house of hee-haw" because of the braying of the donkeys.

"This Lieutenant Siriman Keita . . ." the village chattered. "First his passion for guinea fowls; then he was seized with paternal fondness for an orphan. After that, he fell in love with a hussy. Now his affections run to donkeys. Surely he's crazy?"

"The noise of the cannon, the whistling of the bullets, the snickering of the submachine guns, all that could drive someone mad!"

"Of course he's crazy! He's not normal. Would a sane man have asked a child to choose between a revolver shot to the face and a thrashing, and then adopt him?"

"Have you seen any of our boys go off to carry the rifle for the Whites and not come back acting strange? The people of Kouloubalaya had to clap Fagimba in irons after his demobilization. Now he wanders the village, raving incomprehensibly."

"He wakes up all of Kouloubalaya to the sound of his trumpet, and all day the children march to his command, obeying strict orders and smacks on the head."

Old Soriba was jubilant, often telling of the great trick he'd played on Siriman Keita.

"I harpooned him with one shot, and he didn't even argue."

Day and night, if a single timid bray came from another enclosure, the lieutenant's seven donkeys took it up in chorus. They ran in all directions, and Siriman Keita had to order that his house be better cared for, as an odor of dung assaulted the passersby. And to taunt the lieutenant, the villagers started covering their noses as soon as they saw him. Only the butcher refused to participate in the game.

"You have to understand," he said, "he's my best client. I don't want to lose him. And if he were to set himself up as butcher? He has means that I don't. Mock him as much as you like, but count me out."

Awa started complaining of insomnia from the braying, jumping, and capering. It must be said that the lieutenant didn't joke around in bed.

"The first time," he'd say, "is for fun. The second? Conjugal duty. And the third . . . great contentment and calming of nerves."

The cries of the donkeys slowly harmonized with the daily life of Kouta. They accompanied the rhythm of the talking drum and the steps of the dancers, and served as a wake-up call for the housewives.

One incident, however, provoked a scandal.

The muezzin, woken from his first sleep, hurried off to the mosque and gave the call to prayer. The imam rushed over and pointed a flashlight at him.

"You've gone mad! It's two in the morning."

"I heard the donkeys braying."

"The lieutenant's donkeys!" the imam raged. "That arrogant man who was so impious as to refuse the nuptial blessing!"

He retraced his steps, fuming.

"It won't be said that I've been a bad imam. Tomorrow I'll complain to the commandant of the cercle."

II.

THE IMAM AND THE OTHER ELDERS MET THE NEXT DAY AT THE CERCLE OFFICE. The commandant hadn't yet arrived. His orderly hurried to offer the religious leader a chair and to unfold several mats in the shade of a kapok tree, where the elders took their places. The orderly kept them company, reporting all the cercle gossip.

"For almost a month," he said, "Commandant Bertin, usually the first to arrive, hasn't shown up before nine o'clock. He had a tent set up next to Sobeya on the pretext of going hunting. And what a hunt! He's madly in love with a girl from the village."

"These Whites!" Old Soriba exclaimed. "Whether they're commandants, doctors, or police chiefs, married or single . . ."

His face darkened.

"That Doctor Leroy takes it too far. You know what he did to my youngest wife when she went to the clinic for a checkup?"

"No," the orderly said, his lip hanging.

"Well, he slipped his forefinger . . ."

He stopped and looked around the assembly in the hope that somebody would find a polite expression.

"*Boutou-ba!*" the orderly shouted. "There are no other words for it, Soriba."

"He caressed it at length and then sent her away, saying, 'It doesn't work with this one.' And that's not all . . ."

"The Whites are sneaky!" The orderly burst out laughing. "Doing that with your finger?" He started to sing, stomping a rhythm with his feet: "They come to take our daughters and mistresses from our very embrace. To arms, people of Kouta!"

Everybody laughed at his clowning. The amused guards snapped to attention; one pretended to raise the flag, and the other to play the trumpet.

The orderly turned to Old Soriba.

"I broke the thread of your story: the finger in the *boutou-ba*! Tell me more."

"There is no more!" Old Soriba barked. "I'm talking about something that burns a hole in my stomach, and you're asking for more?"

Then they heard the sound of a motor, and the orderly ran about announcing the commandant's arrival to everyone. Suddenly the cercle office disappeared in a whirlwind of yellow dust. Bertin cut the motor and slammed the car door. A guard ran to take the commandant's rifle and, in his haste, dropped it. The commandant gave him a kick to the kidneys.

"Imbecile! What if it had been loaded?"

"But, Commandant . . ."

"None of this 'But, Commandant'!" Bertin shouted.

The orderly hid himself among the elders.

"He's in a really bad mood this morning," he said. "Ready your questions and answers."

"Perhaps the beauty from Sobeya refused to stretch out on her back, legs in the air, like a dead lizard?" Old Soriba asked vengefully.

Bertin gave his anger free rein, spouting crude insults:

"How did a fuckwit like you end up in the French army?"

"Commandant . . ."

The commandant gave him a violent slap with the back of his hand.

"Bastard! You could have killed me. What if that rifle had been loaded?"

"But it's not, Commandant."

"And how would you know? Oh, these people! No sense of logic whatsoever! It's like my cook. I ask him, N'Dogui, are there any potatoes? He says yes. Are there not any? Yes! Will there be any? Yes! Will there not be any? Yes! It's the only thing they know how to say: yes! And they ask me to train officers to lighten the colonial budget! Yes, Mr. Governor, yes, Mr. Minister of the Colonies, I'll train some officers, but I'll have to kick a lot of ass."

He went into his office, where Leroy, the military doctor, was waiting.

"I'm afraid that the whole region under your administrative responsibility is threatened by a yellow fever epidemic. Could your vaccination have expired?"

"I have no idea, Colonel."

"In that case, I'll drop by your house tonight to vaccinate you."

"Naturally, you'll dine with me."

"With pleasure, Commandant. My cook is sick. Oh, nothing serious! An abortion. You know I don't want to leave anything behind when I have to go."

"Well, until this evening," the commandant said.

Leroy left the office, sharply dressed in his khaki uniform. Old Soriba looked daggers at him, and the doctor, greeting each elder, gave him a broad smile.

From his office, the commandant yelled, "Orderly, send in the imam! Only the imam!"

The religious leader entered, very dignified in his yellow-embroidered burnous. He sat down across from the commandant, who shook his hand.

"Since my posting to Kouta, you're the only dignitary who hasn't come to see me," Bertin said, smiling.

The interpreter translated.

"I kept in close contact with your predecessor," the imam replied. "He was interested in the words of the Prophet and compared them to those of Issa, son of Mariam. We often spent long hours together in discussion. His comments worried and fascinated me all at once."

"Yes, Dotori is an intellectual. I had the honor of serving as his adjunct at Djbo, in Senegal."

He took out his pen and a small notebook.

"Tell me, what can I do for you?"

The imam explained his grievances with calm and distinction, neither raising his voice nor changing his tone.

The interpreter translated:

"He said, Commandant, that the lieutenant's donkeys have become intolerable, and that it would be best to have them sent out of the village. Nobody sleeps in the village anymore."

He stopped and added his own complaints to those of the imam.

"If you'll allow me, Commandant, I'll say that the clerks and the cercle guards also complain of having trouble sleeping because of the donkeys' braying. Then they come late to the cercle office, and the commandant gets angry. But because of the respect that you have for the lieutenant, nobody has ever dared talk to you about it."

"Tell the imam that I'll deal with this personally."

He wrote a note on the spot and then sealed it in an envelope.

"Orderly!"

"Commandant!"

"Go give this letter to the lieutenant."

■   ■   ■

Siriman Keita was dozing in his hammock when the orderly arrived and stood at attention. The lieutenant opened one eye, and then the other.

"Bastard! Son of a bitch!" he howled. "What gives you the right to salute? You've never fired a single bullet! It's a breach of protocol! The cercle guards are one thing, but an orderly? What's the world coming to? I'll speak of this to the commandant of the cercle."

"He's just the one who sent me."

The lieutenant snatched the letter from the orderly's hands, holding his stomach.

"For more than three months, I've been telling Awa: a sheep's head is too heavy for breakfast."

A cramp shook him. He furrowed his brow.

"You there, look at me! I insult your father and your mother, and you don't have the guts to return the favor."

He doubled over in pain.

"Bastard! Call me bastard."

"Bastard," the orderly whispered.

"Son of a bitch! Call me a son of a bitch."

"Son of a bitch," the orderly shouted, as if echoing an order.

"Now you can relax."

The lieutenant appreciated the tone of the message. He read it and reread it, finding it quite pleasant:

Dear Friend,

Would you be so kind as to come down to my office tomorrow at ten o'clock?
I look forward to the pleasure of your visit.

Your devoted friend,
Commandant Jacques Bertin

The lieutenant came exactly on time. At ten o'clock, he stepped onto the
veranda of the cercle office. The cercle guards jumped up and stood at attention.
The orderly thought better of it and held out his hand instead.

"You bastard child! You can't salute like everybody else?"

"You're the bastard child!"

"That insult will cost you dearly," the lieutenant threatened.

"But yesterday morning, Lieutenant . . ."

"That was yesterday," Siriman Keita replied. "And if I allow myself to be
insulted in public, I'll quickly end up as respectable as Togoroko, the village idiot."

The orderly opened the door obsequiously, emphasizing his obedience in
hope of pardon. The commandant rose, smiling generously.

"You came, Lieutenant. And believe me, it's always a pleasure to receive you.
I won't keep you in suspense long. Well, I just nominated you for the Legion
of Honor. I said: 'nominated.' The decision isn't mine to make. However, I'm
very hopeful that the governor will grant my request. No doubt he'll take into
account your growing influence in Kouta. Civil marriage! You set the example,
and since then I've performed a good dozen more. I'd be delighted, next Bastille
Day, to be able to pin the Legion of Honor on this heart that fought for France,
and never stops fighting for her."

He held out a copy of the confidential letter addressed to the governor.

The lieutenant sat down; his head was spinning. He stayed quiet for a long
time.

"First the Croix de Guerre, now the Legion of Honor," he murmured, as if
dreaming.

"But of course, Lieutenant! The Legion of Honor! The crowning achieve-
ment of a life well spent."

The commandant took a moment, searching for the words.

"More and more, the country is shaken by those who talk of independence.
Here, in Kouta, the infection stays hidden. But in Woudi, there is open protest.

They boo me when I make my rounds. I was thinking we could create an incident there and organize a small-scale punitive expedition."

"And who would lead it?"

"Naturally, you, Lieutenant!"

They fell silent. Siriman Keita understood that without wanting to dismiss him, the commandant wished for him to leave. He got up and stood to attention.

"Commandant, I will tell the good news to my friends and Awa."

"Good!"

Instead of returning the lieutenant's salute, the commandant took out his pen, scratched his chin and thought for a moment, looking up at the ceiling.

"Do you have a few more moments to spare? Oh, no more than a minute."

"Of course!"

"The imam came to see me yesterday morning. Oh, I didn't give too much weight to his complaining; however, I'll advise you to send away your donkeys. He could make a fuss about it with the higher-ups, which would compromise our plans."

"I'll send them to my brother in Kouroula."

"You're very wise, Lieutenant."

They shook hands, and through the half-open window, the lieutenant saw the orderly in the courtyard, in lively conversation with a clerk coming back from the latrines.

"I almost forgot," the lieutenant said.

"Yes?"

"Your orderly insulted me earlier."

"Insulted you? Unacceptable! Determine his punishment yourself."

"Guards!" the lieutenant cried.

The two guards dozing on the veranda stood up at the same time. And coming from opposite directions, they ran into each other, heads colliding like two rams, and stumbled to attention, one leaning upon the other.

"Fifteen days of prison for the orderly, with no parole."

12.

THE LIEUTENANT FELL IN LOVE WITH THE VILLAGE OF HIS BIRTH. AT FIRST, he went there to visit his donkeys. Slowly he was captivated by the long dinners accompanied by music, followed by evenings remembering the great deeds of the ancestors. He participated in ritual ceremonies that called on Koutourou and Kassiné, the two protective fetishes of his family. And when the moon was full, the *N'komo*[8] left his hut to the sound of bugles and drums. He threatened the ill-mannered, commanded sacrifices to change the course of the clouds, and proclaimed his power with terrifying screams:

> *A faga jeli*
> *kana bo*
> *fa don a ro*
> *kana maga*
> *kun né la.*

> *I can kill*
> *without spilling blood.*

I can drive a man mad
without touching his brain.

The women and the children hid in their houses, trembling with fear. The N'komo arrived in the village square, welcomed by a formidable pounding of talking drums. The young men, their faces covered with extravagant tattoos or hidden behind animal masks, danced with strong leaps and capers, simulating the gait of the animals they represented, their bodies striped with sweat. The buglers sounded raspy notes, which warned women and children that the N'komo was going to circle the village, looking for witches, before withdrawing.

After this warning, the talking drum thundered from one village to another, while the *N'komojeli*[9] recited:

Sorcerer killer
of great sorcerers!
Eternal legacy of our ancestors,
separate the grain from the chaff,
the chaff from the dust,
for the immortality of our race!
For you,
the foreskins of our male children
returned to the earth.
The millet stalk bends,
its head gleaming with rain,
for the immortality of our race!
Link between those of yesterday and today,
reject the weak!
Shape healthy men
like a sheaf of arrows,
for the immortality of our race!
Command!
And the clouds will burst,
and the millet stalk will always sway,
its head gleaming with rain,
for the immortality of our race!

The audience repeated in chorus:

For you,
the foreskins of our male children
returned to the earth.
The millet stalk bends,
its head gleaming with rain,
for the immortality of our race!

The *N'komo* danced, every muscle unleashed, until his strength was exhausted. Then he rolled on the ground like a madman. Convulsions shook him, then subsided. Lying on the ground, he was no more than the hurried panting of his breath. Two young men carried him on their shoulders back to his hut, as he left behind him his profession of faith:

The Fula is excluded from my company.
The Fula? Excluded forever!
As for the Marka,[10]
may he be taken and his throat cut!
If the Fula is excluded,
may the throat of the Marka be slit.

The people of Kouroula were proud of the respect that the commandant showed Siriman Keita. Each time that the lieutenant wanted to visit, the commandant ordered his chauffeur to drive him. The lieutenant himself decided the day and the hour of his return, and the car came back to collect him.

The lieutenant became the defender of his village's people and soon took over the role of chief. He dispensed justice, authorized divorces, and settled disputes over land sharing. Whenever there was an incident in Kouroula, the elders gathered, uncovered the facts, and sent a messenger to Siriman Keita. He went to the cercle office, explained his desire to go to Kouroula, and the commandant lent him his car.

"You know, my friend," Bertin said, "you're working for me. Ah! If only all the retired soldiers followed your example, the cercle would function better. The cercle guards, in demanding bribes, have lost their authority over the people. Keep this up, Lieutenant, and you'll be canton chief."

The people of Kouta began to complain of the arrogance of those of Kouroula when they arrived in Kouta with their produce on market days. They demanded higher prices than sellers from other villages.

The lieutenant strolled through the market, inflated by his own importance, flanked by two guards armed with *Bougounika*.[11] The people of Kouroula ran to him as he passed, applauding him and singing:

There are three types of sons:
He who doesn't achieve
The renown of his father,
He who equals it,
And he who surpasses it.
Lieutenant Siriman Keita,
Child of Kouroula,
You have pulverized the renown of your ancestors.

The villagers of Kouta said only, "He's an ingrate! He wanted land in our village! A child of our village! A woman of our village! We gave him everything, and he turns against us! The handful of rice has fallen back into the dish and dirtied it."

Only Solo supported the lieutenant.

"My friends," he said. "We must speak the real truth. The truth is like a spicy aftertaste. It pleases no one, the truth. And a man who can't help but speak the truth should have a good horse at hand. Why? To mount it and gallop away after having spoken the truth. Well then, here's the truth, as naked as a girl emerging from the river. All of Kouta's merchants have made their fortunes on the backs of the poor fellows of Kouroula and the neighboring villages. It's only justice that Kouroula has found a protector."

"When God wants to be done with a snake, he takes away its vision," said a merchant.

"But he feeds it," Solo replied.

"Why don't you go live in Kouroula?"

"My homeland is here, and its name is Kouta!"

"You don't know her! You don't love her!"

"Your words are as false as the glass beads that you sell as pearls. I know Kouta so well that I pass through her day and night in darkness. It's true, I haven't liked her since people like you, under the cover of commerce and religion—"

"Scoundrel! Liar!" Daouda shouted from his store.

"Liar? That's true, I am. Remember who you came to six months ago, when you knocked up a seventeen-year-old girl? That day, I was dishonest; otherwise, her parents would have brought you before the commandant."

He stopped, and then continued:

"Ah, these merchants! They've all got comfortable back rooms. Go into a store on market day and ask for the owner. The manager will tell you that he's in the back room. Why? It's what they call a 'quickie,' in exchange for a mirror or a kilo of salt that they offer to a poor country girl."

"That one," Daouda said to himself, "I'll never get even with him."

Solo lashed out, encouraged by the laughter of the spectators who had hurried over.

"All dogs eat shit, but we chase away only the dog that has it on his snout. As for Daouda, he pushed his sin too far."

"What did he do?" asked a man from Kouroula.

"He did it against the wall of the mosque. And to wash this stain from the building, he had to coat it with quicklime, on the advice of the imam."

The lieutenant came to Kouroula one evening, without being summoned, with the three guards who henceforth served as his escort. He had told Awa that he would be away for a few days.

Siriman Keita gathered the people and pronounced imperiously:

"People of Kouroula, from now on you won't have to go to Kouta to pay your taxes. An officer of the cercle will come here to collect them."

The crowd applauded jubilantly.

The lieutenant added, "I've also obtained the commandant's permission to rotate the market between Kouta and Kouroula to save you the trouble of walking ten kilometers every week."

The village showered him with honors. A bull was killed to thank him for the interest he showed in Kouroula, and great celebrations followed the feast.

Faganda could not control the jealousy that gnawed at him.

"Siriman," he said, "you put your hind legs before your front ones. You should've followed custom and asked me to announce the good news to the village; that would have been an honor to our family. Since your demobilization, you've shown me neither consideration nor respect. Today, Kouroula is at your feet, but I'm still the head of my family. So go back to Kouta, and if you ever want to return to Kouroula, don't cross my threshold."

And as the commandant's driver had not been informed, the lieutenant set off walking, singing military marches to persuade himself that he could, at his age and out of shape, manage ten kilometers without a break. He arrived in Kouta late at night. Suddenly, he broke into a forced run. He saw, leaning against the wall of the square house, five bicycles.

The lieutenant went in. He closed the double gate, locked the bicycles in a storeroom, loaded his rifle, and stretched out in his hammock. He heard a burst of laughter.

"I'll change that laughter into screams," he told himself.

A voice sung to the melody of a guitar:

San dibi le y'a ke
nma se bo la
i sobè tè jarabi ma.
Nfa lalen plian rô da la.
Un un! i sobè tè jarabi ma.
Nna tun sobilen.
Un un! i sobè tè jarabi ma . . .

Rain threatened,
I missed our rendezvous.
You don't believe in my love.
My father was asleep
in his chair guarding the door.
No! You don't believe in my love.
My mother is onto us.
But no! You don't believe in my love . . .

"Love! Love!" the lieutenant grumbled. "It's the only word they know. They're worse than the Whites."

An idea came to him; he chased it away. But it came back, haunting him: "What if one of these bushy-haired Zazous was on top of Awa, while the others waited their turn, sitting in my armchairs?"

He rushed into the living room, aimed his rifle, and ordered them to sit on the floor, backs to the wall.

"The first one to try running away gets a bullet in his thigh," he threatened. "Oh! You think my rifle's not loaded? You think I'm joking?"

He aimed at a guinea fowl heading toward the coop and shot it dead. The other members of the household, woken by the shot, came out wrapped in pagnes.

"And nobody ever said anything!" the lieutenant screamed. "Somebody go wake up Bilal right away, and have him come with his tools."

Bilal was a longtime family servant. He lived off of the coins that people gave him for shaving the heads of little boys. In Kouta, no one else would take on such a degrading profession. The children came under his shade hangar, and he could shave ten heads in under an hour. Then he collected the hair and carried it out of the village. No one knew where he buried it.

Bilal came quickly. The lieutenant's summons honored him.

"Let's get right to the point," the lieutenant said, controlling his anger. "Those who want their bicycles back will have their heads shaved. Otherwise, I'll sell them at the next market."

The young men sat one after another, and Bilal worked under the gleam of a flashlight.

"With so little light," he confided to them, "I can guarantee neither the neatness of my work nor the safety of your ears."

When the young men were shaven, the lieutenant ordered them to sit down in a straight line. He went into his bedroom and came back with a vial. Without looking at them, he splashed Mercurochrome on each of their heads.

"It's a disinfectant, and it takes care of wounds."

Then he allowed each one to take his bicycle.

Lying next to his wife, he laughed alone, slapping himself on the stomach. And when Awa ventured a timid caress, he rejected her advances and rolled onto his side. However, he didn't resist the great contentment's call for very long.

■   ■   ■

Solo arrived at the square house for his meal. Since Solo had served zealously, the lieutenant had told him: "I'll feed you, but we'll never eat from the same plate."

Siriman Keita told him the story at length, without omitting the least detail, promising himself he'd tell it again all over Kouta that same evening.

Solo listened, doubled over in laughter.

"Lieutenant, it's been years since I've laughed like that."

Suddenly, he became serious.

"Lieutenant," he said, "you should keep this quiet. Think about your reputation, and Awa's. Consider your renown, growing all across the country. If you'll allow me, I'll suppress this incident and no one will speak of it again."

"Do what you like as long as it doesn't hurt me."

"Ah! Lieutenant, have you ever seen a dog bite the hand that feeds it?"

His meal finished, Solo went to Daouda's store.

"Where is your son?"

"You really despise me, don't you? You could at least follow custom and ask after my health before posing me a question. And what do you want with my son?"

"One question doesn't answer another. And don't tell me that he has an urgent errand to attend to, or that he's in the back room."

He searched for the *tara* with his hands and sat down, sticking his cane up like a question mark.

"Normally, he's the one managing the store. His absence is surprising. Questions are being asked."

He took his time, and then struck.

"Daouda, give it!"

"Give what?"

"Money! Or else I'll expose this business on the next market day."

"You're going to hell, Solo!"

"For sure, we'll be neighbors."

Then he went to the home of Old Soriba, who was eating, surrounded by his wives.

"Has a hyena ever been seen at midday!" the old man called.

"The hyena has come to collect his due," Solo gloated. "And the hyena is always too busy to smoke a pipe. You have to clean it and pack it carefully before blowing your smoke rings. And often it clogs up, swollen with saliva, and the whole operation has to be done again."

Soriba crumpled up three notes of a hundred francs and pressed them into the hand of the blind man, who unfolded them carefully and smelled each one.

"Daouda gave me five of these, and they didn't smell of Mercurochrome."

"Then here are two more, and one extra for your trouble."

"Could you also get Namori the butcher off my back? You're friends. So much so that when he runs out of cattle, you give him donkeys."

"I give you my word."

"In that case, wash your son's head with alcohol, and rub it with methylene blue. I'll tell the whole village that you shaved his head because he had ringworm."

When Solo arrived at the shade hangar of the canton chief, he pretended to stumble and sat down.

"Koulou Bamba, your house smells of Mercurochrome—I'm allergic to it from having spent all my childhood covered in scrapes."

The chief dismissed his courtiers and asked Solo to come in. Solo sat to the right of Koulou Bamba, who greeted him at length.

"How are you?"

"*Ahaba!*"

"And your wife?"

"*Marhaba!*"

"And your children?"

"*Marhaboussé.*"

"You spoke of Mercurochrome, Solo?" the elderly canton chief asked.

"Indeed, Koulou Bamba, if looser tongues than mine got hold of this, your reputation would be sullied. Already your enemies whisper that you're too old to command. Others emphasize your lack of authority, in your home as in the canton. Only a blind man gifted with a big mouth could tell you the truth eye to eye."

"Eye to eye?" Koulou Bamba asked, amused. They laughed together. "How much do you want?"

"I know how generous you are. Even your enemies recognize this quality."

His trick complete, Solo dressed himself in new clothes from head to toe.

"The monkey's bought himself a beautiful knife," people said around the village.

"When a cat buys milk, he drinks it. And he's also a carnivore! If he traps a mouse, he eats it. Let me show off my fine clothes."

"And he's sweating like he was fighting a fire."

"*Bouda ha bou!*[12] Let me strut like a horned viper. Four steps forward! Two steps back! So that everyone can see me at their leisure. *Bouda ha bou!* My stroll only lacks the cheerful voice of a talking drum, to drown out the sound of your farting. Let seven young girls precede me, carrying incense to clear out the smell."

"And what an evil mouth he has! Seven angels coming down from heaven and seven angels heading up met in the middle and threw seven curses on even the greeting from his mouth! And his tongue? They promised to make it the stake on which humans are burned in hell."

"I say, *bouda ha bou*! When the cat buys milk, with his own money, he drinks it. Let me parade my beautiful outfit with my royal horned-viper strut. *Bouda ha bou*, the jealous and envious!"

13.

THAT AFTERNOON, AFTER THE PRAYER, AN EXTRAORDINARY MEETING TOOK place. Kouta's canton chief, the imam, and all of the elders sat in a circle around a young man. He had a black eye, a bloody lower lip, a sprained ankle, a skull covered in wounds, and his left arm in a sling.

"Now, Maliki, speak," Koulou Bamba said. "We're listening. But remember that an eloquent speech is not always a true one."

This setting intimidated the young man. He struggled to pull himself together, looked nervously around at the elders, and crafted his expression to win their sympathy.

"I arrived Wednesday evening at Woudi to sell my kola nuts at the market the following day. Sambou, the son of Bakou—who's hosted me for as long as we've known each other—informed me his father wished that I never again cross their threshold. I went to sleep in the mosque."

"You did the right thing," said the imam. "But without wishing to cast doubt on your words, I'm surprised that Bakou, a respected village chief and a good Muslim, would make such a decision."

This remark disconcerted Maliki. He wiped his lip with a blood-spotted handkerchief and adjusted his sling, grimacing in pain.

"After the morning prayer, I went to the marketplace. And to my great astonishment, all the vendors refused to sell me millet cakes and porridge. Soon the market began. I found a seller from Woudi in my usual spot, and he refused to give it up. I showed him the ticket that assigned me that spot, not far from Bakou's house. He answered by spitting. So I rented another spot."

He took out his wallet and passed the blue ticket around so that each could see and touch it.

"It's the truth," Daouda said. "This ticket was issued by the director of Woudi market on Thursday, which is today."

Indignation showed on several faces.

"I didn't know you were so patient," said Old Soriba.

"A speech is like a string," Daouda intervened. "Let's not cut it with useless remarks."

"I would say," Old Soriba replied, "that speech is like millet cakes. They must be taken one after another until the last, upon which all of the others rested. And this last one is truth."

"What I said and what you're saying? Fish from the same river."

Koulou Bamba put an end to their oratorical joust.

"Let's not break the string or scare off the fish. Let Maliki finish his story."

"The market was in full swing. A group of young people came over to me. One of them walked on the kola nuts that I had displayed in a basket. Another took a nut, cracked it open, and spit red saliva in my face. Then I let my anger get the best of me."

"Anger, even just anger, distorts things," the imam emphasized.

"And if somebody walked on an open Koran before your eyes?" Solo asked.

"I would leave it to God and his Prophet."

"Pathetic!" cried Solo. "May those with no one to count on resort to God!"

"You've spoken well," said Magassi approvingly.

He was the youngest of the elders. He had a tuft of hair atop his head, and people said that if you so much as brushed against it, he would rip out your nose hairs. In fact, he was allowed to sit on the council of elders to channel and moderate his combative tendencies.

"Let Maliki finish his story," the canton chief said, getting impatient.

"Alone against ten young men, I don't know what happened after that. But I remember their shouts: 'Death to the people of Kouta! Sellouts to the Whites! Long live independence!'"

"There are cercle guards in Woudi," Koulou Bamba said, astounded. "What did they do?"

"They didn't intervene!"

The canton chief dismissed Maliki with a gesture of his hand. Maliki left, leaning heavily on his crutch. To the passersby who asked:

"The people of Woudi," he said. "There were ten of them beating me as I lay on the ground. And the cercle guards there didn't come to my aid. It was a plot, and if you ignore a plot, it's because it was woven in your presence."

.   .   .

The meeting continued in closed session.

"Speech is like a banquet, and when a banquet is served, each should take his part."

"True!" Solo added. "It doesn't make sense to leave the drum circle and dance alone around a courtyard, beating your chest."

"I think that Maliki was assaulted," said Old Soriba. "But what should we do?"

"It's time we freed ourselves from Woudi's arrogance!" Magassi shouted.

His fist hammered his thigh as if pummeling an imaginary enemy.

"Let the Fula minority, to whom we've given asylum, act like the masters of our land? No! It's intolerable!"

"Since Woudi gained in importance, trade has slowed in Kouta," Daouda said. "It would be proper to reestablish Kouta's supremacy over the surrounding villages."

Solo lit the fuse:

"Sellouts to the Whites! Have you already forgotten the scorn of that accusation? Oh, the Fula! If you see a Fula, wait to see his double. And what's his double? Treachery!"

"This calls for an expedition!" Magassi shouted.

"Not that," the imam said. "For goodness' sake; for the love of God!"

"The Prophet Mamadou, would he be Prophet if he hadn't conquered by force?" Solo asked. "Well, I'll tell you this: I'm ready to carry the flag for Kouta."

"A blind man, going off to war?" Daouda joked.

"Do you remember, in the circumcision hut, when you were being taken care of and shouting loud enough to draw the whole village—who gagged you?"

"You're going to get mad at me the one time we agree?"

Koulou Bamba rose, looking worried.

"In my role as canton chief, I neither can nor should favor one village. Let's get the commandant's opinion."

■   ■   ■

Commandant Bertin received the elders grudgingly. He listened to Koulou Bamba recount Maliki's misadventures without lifting his head. And when the canton chief had finished explaining the facts:

"I'm up to my neck in quarrels both within Kouta and between Kouta and its neighbors. You're going to drive me crazy in the end."

He stood up, signaling the end of the conversation.

"Guards, send in the next one."

"Commandant," Koulou Bamba insisted, "certain minds are very excited, and I'm very concerned that armed conflict could break out between Kouta and Woudi."

Bertin shrugged his shoulders, cracked his knuckles nervously.

"Do what you like . . ."

Then his anger took over and he gave himself to it without restraint.

"Surely you know that the supporters of independence are gaining more and more followers? Fine then, we'll leave this country. Oh, I have nothing to fear. I'll leave, my pith helmet under my arm. And when the country is torn apart by tribal wars, you'll call for us again. Then I'll be back with the same helmet, but on my head this time."

He opened the door to his office himself, and then turned to the imam:

"The sacred text of the sura forbids that the host or his guest depart in haste, but I have much to do."

"No matter," the imam murmured, bowing slightly. "We'll do as you wish."

He left the office, followed by the other elders.

Solo appeared at the square house well before the noon meal. The lieutenant was dozing, stretched out in his hammock. Solo sat beside him in silence, without waking him. Some moments later, Siriman Keita opened his eyes, yawned elaborately, and sat up in his hammock, pinching his nose.

"Since you bought those new clothes, I can smell you a mile away," he grumbled.

"The man who walks much, sweats much," Solo retorted. The remark had irritated him. "And a man shouldn't always smell of soap or cologne. It's a sign of laziness."

The lieutenant yawned again and rubbed his eyes.

"You're early for the meal. The servants have hardly gotten back from the market."

"I was sent to you, Lieutenant."

"By whom?" Siriman Keita asked excitedly.

"The elders."

"They have so little respect for me that, instead of coming themselves, they send me an old blind man that I feed!"

He lay down again, closed his eyes, and pretended to fall back asleep.

"Lieutenant, Kouta wants to mount an expedition against Woudi."

"An expedition? And why? Just more of your scheming."

"It's the truth, Lieutenant. The people of Woudi beat up Maliki, a young merchant that the commandant holds in high esteem. You told me, in confidence . . ."

"I know," the lieutenant interrupted.

"At the council of the elders, following your wish, I added hot water to what was already in the pot. It rose slowly, and the pot boiled over."

"And the canton chief, what did he say?"

"Too old to make a decision."

"The commandant?"

"Your question is an insult to my father and mother. Kouta is on her knees before you. And if the expedition succeeds, you will be the chief of the canton, or commandant when the Whites leave the country. The man who coughs never loses; if he doesn't spit, he swallows. You're in a position of strength."

"The Whites, leaving the country! Never repeat that again in my house, or you can forget about coming here. No! Who would pay my pension?"

A juvenile excitement ran through him. He saw himself armed with a flyswatter, sitting on the skin of a three-year-old bull, surrounded by courtiers and griots singing his praises.

"Go to the elders at once. Tell them I'm waiting for them so that we can finalize a plan of attack."

"Of course! And they'll come. If you tell a blind man, 'Come, I'm going to give you eyes,' he'll come. And a paralytic asks only to be carried."

The lieutenant launched into a monologue:

"Desperate times call for desperate measures! All's fair in love and war, except losing. Let each man arm himself as best he can. The merchants' trucks have been requisitioned for our transport. We leave for Woudi tomorrow at dawn. Nothing beats the element of surprise."

∎   ∎   ∎

The trucks hummed along single file in the cool morning air. The lieutenant stood tall in the back of the first truck, chest puffed out, waist cinched with a cartridge belt. He had tightened his helmet, fearing the wind might carry it away. From time to time, he kicked the driver's cab to urge him to go faster. Every fifteen minutes, he checked his watch, turned, and peered through the yellow dust to see if the three other trucks were still in the convoy he'd created.

Two kilometers from Woudi, the lieutenant called the convoy to a halt and divided his force into two columns.

"We'll go the rest of the way on foot," he said. "The first column will attack under my command, and the second will join us in half an hour, when I whistle. Strike! Show no mercy! This is war. But be warned: if you so much as think about raping a woman, I'll put you down with my rifle, point-blank."

The lieutenant took the village without meeting the slightest resistance. He had the women and children shut in their homes and ordered that each man be given twenty lashes. He forced Bakou to kneel before him and beg for mercy, promising that there would no longer be a market in Woudi. The village chief accepted all their conditions. Then Magassi pissed in a bowl and poured it onto Bakou's head.

"Now we'll affirm the supremacy of Kouta over all of the villages that come to Woudi's market."

"That wouldn't be wise," advised Old Soriba.

"I'm in charge here!" the lieutenant snapped.

They took Barani without a fight. The people of Dougouni received them as heroes and promised to never frequent Woudi's market again. For defending themselves, the people of Kolonni each earned ten strokes of the whip.

On the return trip, at the entrance to Woudi, they saw two tree trunks lying across the road.

"Let's get some volunteers up there to move them!" the lieutenant yelled.

At that moment, an explosion rang out, followed immediately by a war song:

Fila ni maninka
bilara nyogon na
Fila ye maninka mina
k'o kili ci.

Tiya le tiya le
Fila ni maninka
mana bila nyogon na
Fila na maninka mina
k'a dondon.

The Fula and the Mandinka
have fought.
The Fula took the Mandinka
and castrated him.

It's true! It's true!
Every time the Fula
and the Mandinka fight,
the Fula takes the Mandinka
and always castrates him.

"First column, attack!" the lieutenant ordered.

A hail of rocks from slingshots battered the trucks.

"My truck!" Daouda complained. "They broke the windows of my truck."

"First column, fall back!" the lieutenant shouted.

The clearing caught fire, and the blaze, driven by the wind, swept toward the people of Kouta.

"The battle is lost!" Old Soriba wailed. "I knew this would happen."

And as if to silence him, a projectile struck him in the mouth. He held one tooth in his hand and did his best not to swallow another.

"Retreat!" cried the lieutenant.

But the whipped and conquered people of the other villages had gathered and were marching on them, cutting off their retreat.

"Boubacar Diallo," the lieutenant said, "you're Fula. Better than anyone, you can negotiate with Bakou."

"Our families have been enemies for many years, ever since an old quarrel."

"I'll go myself," boasted the lieutenant.

At the entrance to Woudi, two men lifted him from the ground; when he struggled, another tied him up, and they threw him at Bakou's feet.

Bakou pulled out his knife and grabbed hold of the lieutenant's member.

"Shout, 'Long live independence!'—or else."

"Long live independence."

"Here is your helmet, the symbol of your submission to the Whites. Crush it under your foot."

The lieutenant did so.

"Have him locked in a hut," the chief ordered. "And don't give him anything to eat or drink. His companions can go back to Kouta, but on foot."

At the exit to the village, the women rushed about with calabashes overflowing with cow dung, which they poured onto the fleeing men.

Bakou put on a colossal performance of talking drums to celebrate the victory. To the village's great satisfaction, a group of clowns imitated the rout of Kouta's men, contorting themselves extraordinarily, grimacing and making obscene gestures. The young people added their own rhythm to the great victory dance, forming long, curving lines.

And when their excitement gave way to fatigue, at a sign from Bakou, the drummers stopped. The war song resumed, accompanying the fleeing men of Kouta:

> *The Fula and the Mandinka*
> *have fought.*
> *The Fula took the Mandinka*
> *and castrated him.*

The next day, Kouta's market was teeming with people when a truck appeared, traveling at high speed. The driver braked in the center of the Dotori Bridge and reversed, engine howling. He backed into the crowd, honking nervously, and stopped in front of the butcher's.

Two men lowered the lieutenant from the truck while two others, armed with rifles, kept the crowd at bay. Only a wide loincloth stood between Siriman Keita and nudity. The merchants ran to him, their boubous spread, trying to shield him from the gaze of the women.

He shut himself in his square house to chew over his humiliation and rancor. Sometimes Solo paid him a visit, bringing him the latest gossip. The lieutenant listened with a vague and absent look. Solo would take his leave, saying to himself: "That's one broken man! He'll never be the same again."

Awa no longer appeared at the market, fearing that certain women would spout their bile about the state of her husband. She passed long hours in Siriman's company, but at the end of all her lovely reasoning, the lieutenant would answer, "Not all of the dead are underground. Humiliation is worse than death."

■   ■   ■

One morning, the commandant's orderly appeared at the square house. He knocked heavily at the gate. Awa came to open it.

"On behalf of the commandant," he said, holding out a summons for the lieutenant.

The lieutenant read: "Lieutenant Siriman Keita is summoned to the commandant's office for an affair that concerns him."

The orderly opened a logbook and gave the lieutenant a pencil. He signed next to his name without betraying the least sign of anxiety.

"And when should I present myself?"

"Right away," the orderly responded.

"Good! Give me a moment to pack my bag, and I'll follow you."

Commandant Bertin made the lieutenant wait on the veranda, sitting on a bench. The guards barely greeted him. The orderly taunted him: "Yesterday an elephant, today a hare! Let me tell you, it's the wisdom of our ancestors: don't lie on your back and shoot piss in the air. Some drops will fall back on your own stomach."

"Send in Lieutenant Siriman Keita!" the commandant shouted.

He didn't rise, but indicated a chair and got straight to the point.

"You have to understand: I'm a civil servant, an underling. And an underling must realize what he is. Well, I just received a telegram from the governor ordering me to arrest you for disturbing the peace. Believe me, I'm terribly upset."

"Remember, Commandant, you're the one who had the idea of a punitive expedition against the people of Woudi, and you plotted all this with Maliki, the cercle guards of Woudi, and me myself."

"What are you saying, lieutenant! You're accusing me? Look, he's accusing me! I'm going to refer this to the governor!"

Trembling with rage, he took an enormous file, leafed through it at length, and took out a typed page bearing the label "Confidential."

"Here are the minutes of the meeting that I had with the elders when they told me of the dispute between Kouta and Woudi. Naturally, as a good administrator, I sent a copy up the ladder. Do you want me to read it to you?"

"No, that won't be necessary."

"Very well."

His face tensed. He looked the lieutenant square in the face.

"Guards!"

"Could I make one request?"

"Always."

"Please, no handcuffs."

"You insult me, Lieutenant. I would never have done such a thing. And for good reason! You've served France. You'll sleep at the prison. It's the law. And you'll leave tomorrow morning for Darako, where you'll be judged."

14.

THE TRAIN STOPPED AT KOUTA'S STATION, AND A MAN STEPPED DOWN FROM the last car. He had only one small bag for luggage. He avoided the crowd coming to meet friends and relatives, and took a shortcut toward the village.

The hot noise of the night market came to him, and he hesitated.

"If they see me, too bad," he said to himself. "I've made my decision."

The lieutenant entered the market, shook people's hands, and gave news of his health to those who asked. And when they spoke of his time in prison, he simply answered, "Every man has two houses: the one he built with his own hands, and the one that his life's misadventures built for him. I had a debt toward all those who, consciously or not, suffered from my deeds. I have paid it."

When he arrived at the square house, fear or shame kept him from knocking. Hearing footsteps, Famakan asked, "Who is it?"

"It's me, your father."

The young man threw back the bolt and rushed into his father's arms, his eyes misty with tears. He struggled to hold them back, but his voice betrayed his emotion.

"A man shouldn't cry," the lieutenant scolded.

Awa appeared, wrapped in a white sheet. To the lieutenant's excited greetings, she lowered her head. In her eyes, Siriman saw a fear that she could not control. Her gestures were abrupt, and her voice shook.

"You're expecting a child?" In his voice, there was neither anger nor wounded pride.

She started to cry, striking herself in the chest.

"No," the lieutenant said, "don't do that! The neighbors will hear, and they'll think I've beaten you."

He took her by the hand and led her to the living room.

"The father—who is the father of your child?"

"A young man from Darako who comes here to speak on independence, to urge people to vote 'No' in the next referendum."

"Independence . . . They talk about it even in prison, and it would be a good thing for everybody."

And for the first time, Awa saw tears in the eyes of the man who had seemed carved from stone.

"I'm excluded from this happiness. Disqualified, from the very beginning, Siriman Keita."

He took a cup, filled it, and quenched his thirst.

"You've failed one of your responsibilities as my wife. Water! Bring me a little water after six months in prison."

A paternal tone crept into his voice.

"This young man, is he here tonight, with you?"

"Yes."

"Then, good night."

．　　．　　．

The imam entered the courtyard of the square house. The man who greeted him seemed transformed, his face thin, as if after a long illness or interior struggle.

The lieutenant drew out the greetings endlessly, asking for news of everyone:

"And our canton chief?"

"We've had the misfortune of losing him; his wives are still in mourning."

"He was a good chief."

"Indeed," the imam agreed. "He knew how to take the advice of others. And while it's always good form to praise the dead, I swear before God that I don't remember a single thing that I could hold against him."

Silence settled over them.

"When I left prison," the lieutenant said, "I faced a serious problem. Perhaps you've already heard the rumor?"

The imam didn't answer.

"My wife is expecting a child that can't be mine."

"The mother is always known, but no one can ever say for sure, 'this is my father.'"

"I intend to recognize the child as my own." His face tensed up with worry. He resisted it and forced a smile. "Is my decision wise?"

"I believe so, Lieutenant. We've seen you feed an orphan and love him as if you yourself had brought him into the world."

The imam started to stand, cracking his joints. The lieutenant held him by a fold of his boubou.

"I still have another, more serious decision to discuss with you."

"I'm listening. He who listens reaps the rewards."

"I'm joining the great Muslim community."

"I knew you'd come to us. You see, Lieutenant, when God calls someone, he asks for neither his father's name, nor that of his mother. But think about it some more; allow your decision time to ripen. Islam is a beautiful religion, but a demanding one."

"Don't call me 'Lieutenant,'" he said with a touch of irony, as if mocking himself. "The lieutenant died."

"In prison?"

"No, long before! On the day that a white doctor told him that he could never impregnate a woman. And all the wrong that the lieutenant did to others was just to prove to himself he wasn't dead."

"Will you be able to forget the evil your wife has done to you?"

"I have known evil, and I have left it. It no longer exists to me."

"What is evil, after all?"

"Perhaps it is to never change?"

The imam's face radiated joy, and he almost fell on his knees before the lieutenant in taking his leave.

■   ■   ■

The conversion ceremony was held the next morning. Bilal, coming at dawn, had shaved the lieutenant and slaughtered a ram. The women of the neighborhood helped Awa around a huge cauldron of corn porridge. Resting in his chair, the lieutenant waited, beaming like a man transformed.

The imam announced himself from afar, reciting verses of the Koran, which his disciples then took up in unison. Once he had crossed the threshold, Old Soriba came to meet him and cleared a path for him to a mat spread in the center of the audience. The imam took his place, while his disciples continued to chant the passages from the Holy Book dedicated to the ceremony.

On the imam's signal, they fell silent, and the lieutenant came to crouch before him. The imam gave the lieutenant half a kola nut, which he chewed. Eyes closed, the religious leader put both hands on the lieutenant's shaved head, inviting all the audience to recite the Fatiha seven times.

The women sent around calabashes of sweet porridge, which the people ate in small circular groups. The imam and the elders excused themselves, taking their share of the ram, while Awa, mobbed by the griots, distributed pagnes, silver, and jewelry.

The lieutenant was no longer seen, except around noon on Fridays, when, at the muezzin's call, he left the square house for the great prayer, dressed in white, with a large, multicolored parasol, its handle circled in gold, protecting him from the sun. Famakan, neatly dressed, followed him, holding a red-bordered sheepskin.

The lieutenant began avoiding the market, and when he did go there, it was to get coins, which he then gave to poor people begging for food.

When the household chores allowed it and she was pure, Awa accompanied her husband, her head covered with a white scarf to shield her face from the curiosity of passersby and other women, who felt a combination of admiration, jealousy, and envy for her. The lieutenant always spread his sheepskin prayer mat in the same place, far from the imam. Awa took a spot in the area reserved for women.

The lieutenant and the imam had developed a friendship that they maintained at a certain distance. It drew its strength from their discretion and mutual trust. Each time that the imam noticed that his friend hadn't come to the Friday prayer, he paid him a visit that same evening. They talked at length on problems of faith and the dedication of oneself to God. And often, when a delicate question troubled the imam, a marriage or a divorce that was difficult to settle, he consulted the lieutenant.

After the Friday prayer, the elders divided into two groups. One stayed in front of the mosque to discuss the life of the village. The other accompanied the lieutenant to the square house, where Awa served tea and Solo enlivened it with long, animated conversations. Even though the lieutenant didn't like the subject, they talked more than anything about independence.

"Independence," Solo would often say, "you don't know what it will mean. I'll tell you: a great banquet."

The lieutenant nodded his head.

"Rich and poor will be invited."

"As for me," the lieutenant joked, "I'll be demoted."

"You'll lose nothing, Siriman. The rich will eat, and once they're full, they'll wipe their oily hands on the mouths of the poor."

The lieutenant tried to change the subject.

"I'd very much like to build a mosque in Kouroula and set up a marabout there to convert my brothers."

Solo went back on the attack with still greater force. "Independence would mean equality, the propagandists say." Addressing Daouda: "The merchants will beg for mercy because the peanut trade will be nationalized."

"And the blind?"

"The wind that fells the mortar doesn't spare the pestle."

"If the commandant heard you, he would surely kiss you," Siriman snickered.

When the sun began the last quarter of its journey, the group returned to the mosque and reunited with the others.

They criticized the young people's behavior and the Zazou style, with its tight, form-fitting pants.

"When you pray," the imam said, "the forehead should touch the ground. With their hair sticking out in a bouquet like that, God cannot accept their prayers."

"Daouda," Old Soriba said, "your son might as well just walk around naked. The other day, he passed in front of my house while I was eating. And the youngest of my wives had to turn her head, shouting: '*Bissimilaï!*' His buttocks were separated in two. And in front, he was showing off a bulge as big as an orange."

They also criticized the women who showed, more and more, too much of their bodies: the back nude, the chest jutting forward, supported by a stuffed bra. And everyone railed against the band that kept the whole village awake each Saturday.

And that was why, after the evening prayer, you could hear insults and curses around Kouta, accompanied by stick blows; the lieutenant's conversion had become a weapon that everyone used to fight the degradation of morals and the disintegration of the family.

Solo, clearing a path for himself through the dark, stopped before each household. "Independence will come sooner or later. He who opposes the inevitable sweats in the rain."

15.

THE OLD MUEZZIN DIED ONE MORNING AT FIVE O'CLOCK. THE DAY BEFORE, he'd received a telegram announcing the arrival of his brother, who had left fifteen years before to seek his fortune in Sierra Leone. All day long, the muezzin had carried the good news from house to house under a crushing sun. That evening he was taken with fever, and it worsened in the night. His temples burned. He forced himself to drink a little sweet porridge and go to sleep. When his alarm clock sounded at four-thirty, he labored to stand up, soaked in sweat, reeling with vertigo.

"I have to go," he told himself. "Otherwise they won't come to prayer."

Arriving at the mosque, he climbed up the stairs of the minaret. Each step weakened him more.

"*Allah akbar!*" he said once, twice.

Suddenly he felt his head spinning and lost his footing. He had the strength to say "*Allah*" once more and then collapsed.

The imam didn't hear the rest of the call to prayer. He stopped his ablutions and hurried to the mosque. The muezzin had fallen head-first from the minaret. His heart was still beating as the imam carried him like a child and laid him on a mat inside the mosque.

He finished the call himself, performed the prayer, and recited over the muezzin's body the suras for a man's death.

After the burial, the elders held a meeting.

"We need another muezzin," the imam said. "It's a difficult task, and only a man who's completely available can perform it well. If there are no volunteers, I await your suggestions. But as you know, the imam has the authority to choose the man that he thinks most capable of fulfilling the role."

"The lieutenant, who is retired and has no material worries, would be a good muezzin," Old Soriba said.

"I was thinking of him," the imam agreed.

"I'm but a novice among you," Siriman Keita protested.

"A novice?" The imam was astonished. This man, who normally suggested more than spoke, now became passionate. "A novice among us?" he repeated, almost furious. "No, God knows no neophytes. And if you were one, perhaps he'd be touched to have his glory proclaimed five times a day by a novice."

He stopped and thought for a moment:

"There are some deeds that one must remember at the proper time: we have seen you forgive an adulterous wife. And if I scratch at a poorly healed wound, I ask your pardon."

He raised his eyes to Siriman, two tears falling into his white beard.

"I'm your imam, and from father to son, men of my family have held this position since the founding of Kouta."

He glared at the elders, as if to convince them in advance.

"And I swear before God that nobody here would have been capable of such a gesture."

His head lowered, his voice cracking: "Not even your imam," he murmured, crying. "The imam would have taken refuge in tradition and repudiated Awa. But if the imam, upon his deathbed, could designate his successor, you would have been his choice."

And in a tone that allowed no reply:

"Siriman, you will be my muezzin. I have spoken!"

.　.　.

Daouda entered the vestibule of Old Soriba, who was busy eating. The two men were more accomplices than friends and supported each other in the council of elders. Before each meeting, they met to coordinate their efforts, and each intervened to support the proposals of the other. They were never seen side by side. When Daouda made a mistake in an argument, Old Soriba flashed him a prearranged sign and took up the attack.

"Come eat," Old Soriba said now, snatching up a large chunk of meat and stuffing it in his mouth.

"I have already honored the cooking of my own wives."

"Well, come eat your fill."

"Eat my fill? You're saying there's not enough to eat at my house?"

"I was saying things just to tease you."

He took another piece of meat and pushed the plate over to Daouda.

"Do me a favor and taste it."

"Taste it? Are you denying the culinary talents of my wives?"

"Since you're so sensitive, I order you to finish this plate. I speak as your elder."

Daouda did so.

"What's going on? I always fear the visitor who comes at mealtimes."

Daouda started to laugh.

"Afraid that he'll accept your invitation?"

"It's the truth!" Old Soriba confirmed. "They're the ones that come at noon, under the pretext of an urgent message, to take off their dry shoes in front of your house. You invite them to share your meal. They refuse the first invitation, giving in already to the second, and just like that, the plate's empty. Neither you nor they are satisfied. You played that trick on me less than a week ago; that's why your visit scared me. As for Solo, before Siriman started feeding him, well, as soon as he came into my house, I'd burp as loud as I could to convince him that I'd already finished my meal."

The two men laughed, clapping each other on the back.

"I got rid of Solo another way," Daouda said. "I eat in my bedroom."

"The bedroom!" cried Old Soriba. "The aroma of the dish mixes with the smell of the incense."

"And when he arrives, my wives tell him that I'm already asleep."

"Now I understand why he tells everybody that you suffer from sleeping sickness," Old Soriba said. He washed his hands, wiped his mouth, and belched. "We're worse than our wives. Tell me, what leads you to my door?"

"The young *talibé* that I give room and board to has just revealed to me some of the imam's plans."

"What are they?"

"The month of Ramadan is approaching, and the imam intends to appoint one of us as town crier."

"For as long as I can remember, in Kouta it's always been the muezzin who, before the call to prayer, goes door to door waking those who wish to participate in Ramadan."

"The imam thinks that Siriman is growing weak," Daouda said. "I've come up with the perfect plan."

"What?"

"Right before, I'm going to fake a sudden fever. And you, you will go to the meeting very late."

"And what reason will I give to excuse myself?"

"I know you're smart enough to come up with something plausible."

"In truth, Daouda, it's a good scheme. I'd even say it's flawless."

. . .

Old Soriba was the first to the meeting, arriving before even the imam, who complimented him. And when all of the elders were present, he asked to speak.

"The young *talibé* who lives with Daouda told him that the imam wants a volunteer to lighten the muezzin's load during the month of Ramadan. Daouda was so pleased by the news that he developed a fever and refused the dish that my wives had prepared especially for him: fonio with fresh okra. And though sick, he's asked me to let you know that he volunteers for this noble task."

"A merchant?" Seydou exclaimed.

"We merchants have much to be forgiven for."

"In that case, I've bothered you all for nothing," the imam said, adjourning the meeting.

At that moment, the commandant's orderly appeared, riding his bicycle at full speed. Without getting off his bike, he handed a sealed letter to the lieutenant.

"A summons from the commandant," he said.

"What does he want with you?" the imam asked, concerned.

"I don't know."

"When do you have to go there?"

"Since it doesn't mention a time or a day, I suppose it's about something urgent."

"In that case, I'm coming with you."

Commandant Bertin was pacing about the veranda. When he saw the imam and the lieutenant, he came to greet them with a big smile.

"My dear friend," he said to the lieutenant, "would you be so kind as to come into my office?"

"May the imam be present for our meeting?"

"But of course, lieutenant! I know you're friends. He'll share your joy. Joy grows when it's shared."

The commandant sat down behind his table, smiling and cheerful.

"Here it is, your Legion of Honor. The governor has granted my request."

He took out a confidential letter and handed it to the lieutenant.

"Read it yourself. Not only have you been made a Knight of the Legion of Honor, but they also offer their apologies. After an inquiry, it turns out you were falsely accused. Look at the last paragraph: an invitation to return to France, to Fréjus, Marseille, Toulon, where you'll be received by other retired soldiers that you know. Naturally, I'll need to fix a date with you for the ceremony. For my part, I was thinking of the eleventh of November—that is to say, in less than a month."

"After my arrest, I wrote a letter to some of my friends in France to inform them of the humiliation that I endured."

The commandant cracked his knuckles nervously.

"They intervened!" the lieutenant crowed.

He folded the letter and, with a calculated slowness, gave it back to the commandant. Then he stood up.

The imam took hold of his boubou.

"No, Siriman," he said, "don't do that. You must never humiliate someone. That would be pride, and you would disappoint me."

The lieutenant sat down again.

"You know, Lieutenant, that incident in Woudi, it was the independence movement that lodged those complaints about you, and in high places. And the governor ordered your arrest out of fear that the country would be torn apart by internecine wars."

"Never mind that, Commandant. I accept the invitation from my brothers-in-arms. But as for the Legion of Honor, I ask that you return it to the governor."

"Think it over, Lieutenant! That would be an insult to France."

"I have, Commandant. I have thought it over."

The orderly, who had listened to the whole conversation, his ear glued to the door, asked if he could walk with the lieutenant and the imam.

"Siriman," he said jubilantly, "you struck him to the core. And he'll take his anger out on us."

"Bastard! Son of a bitch! Say it to me: son of a bitch."

"Son of a bitch!" the orderly shouted.

"So we're even, then," said the lieutenant, giving him a friendly nudge.

The imam smiled and turned a disdainful look on the cercle office.

Alone inside, Bertin mourned the sad conclusion to his career.

"Orderly! Guards!"

"Commandant!"

"Sir!"

"Commandant . . ."

"Tell N'Dogui to bring me the bottle of Berger with some water, lots of water."

16.

THE VILLAGE WAS SEIZED BY THE NEWS. THE WOMEN STOOD AT THEIR FENCES, passing it along from one household to the next.

"Bintou, did you hear the news?"

"What news?"

"Well, our muezzin . . ."

"Don't tell me . . ."

"A dog bit him this morning."

Bintou, in turn, passed it on.

"Fatou, did you hear what happened during the night?"

"When I'm asleep, not even the thunder would know how to wake me."

"The lieutenant, I mean, our muezzin . . ."

"I don't want to hear the rest."

"This morning, a mad dog bit him in the calf."

"*Ndeissane!*"[13]

Fatou slipped through a hole that the children had made in the fence and came to sit beside Amy.

"Is your husband asleep?"

"When he spends the night with me, he sleeps, despite the aphrodisiacs you got me. I put them in his food and even in the water that I bring him after his meal. But when it's my night, Soriba sleeps."

"Did you hear the news?"

"You fibber!"

"Our muezzin . . ."

"On such a beautiful morning, *eh ndamansa*![14] Peace to your mouth!"

"Bitten by a dog."

"Where?"

"As he was leaving the mosque."

"That part I knew. I meant, what part of his body? The calf, they're saying?"

"No, higher, Amy! Higher!"

"In the thigh?"

"Higher still."

"So the dog got a mouthful of those things that clatter against each other when a man is standing?"

"Exactly!"

"Reckless dog, *ndeissane*!"

She clapped her hands together and looked dismayed.

"What a shame and what great misfortune! If only it had attacked Soriba. But, of course, when it's my night, even the call of the muezzin can't wake him, and yet we live right next to the mosque."

"It's luck, Amy."

"Poor Awa!"

"Yes, poor Awa!"

"You'd be happy in her place."

"She'll have to take a lover."

"What are you saying, Amy? She wasn't expecting this misfortune . . ."

"*Eh nba!*"[15]

Her lip hanging, her eyes sparkling, Amy waited.

"Whatever you do, don't tell this to anybody. You hear me, Amy? You mustn't."

"This is how little you trust me! We've been friends since we were children. Have I even once spread a secret you've confided in me?"

Faking indignation, she rose and went back under her shade hangar, where she busied herself stirring a boiling pot of millet paste.

"It's just advice and nothing more," Fatou apologized. "A little gossip here, a little gossip there, the conversation heats up, and suddenly a secret is revealed."

"Keep your secret!" Amy shouted without turning.

"We're not going to get mad at each other over something so small, are we?" Her voice quiet, as if fearing an indiscreet ear was listening: "If we're to believe Solo, Daouda and Awa are, as the saying goes, like honey and porridge."

Amy laughed mockingly, clapping her hands; took Fatou by the shoulder; and said with feigned compassion: "*Nba!* So you're already rivals without having the same husband? *Ndeissane!*"

∎   ∎   ∎

That evening the imam and the other elders paid a visit to the lieutenant. Awa was sitting at his bedside while the nurse monitored a blood transfusion.

"He's lost a lot of blood," he said. "But don't worry; I'm going to fix him up, and we'll hear his voice waking the village again soon. Don't worry at all; his life is in no danger."

"By the grace of God!" the imam said.

Having heard the rumor, Faganda came to Kouta. He demanded to be left alone with his brother.

"Siriman," he said, "everyone mocked you when you fell off your horse. You're the only member of our family to see the inside of a prison. And you took your pride so far as to offend us by giving our family name to some bastard child. A dog's bite is a sure sign of a curse. You brought this misfortune upon yourself, and if I weren't so forgiving, I'd say that you earned it for abandoning the beliefs of your ancestors."

He paused and looked sternly at the lieutenant.

"When you give birth to a snake, you make a belt of it. Also, I've sacrificed to Koutourou and Kassiné, the protective fetishes of our family. They trampled on my offerings. The two red roosters died in frantic convulsions, on their left sides, turned toward the west, where the sun sets."

He took the lieutenant's hand as if to get his full attention.

"So I consulted the *N'komo*. For a whole night, he threatened: 'From my urine arose the caiman that bit me. The child that I baptized and protected has rebelled against me.' I sacrificed a black billy goat, his favorite animal, and then a three-year-old bull. Finally appeased, the *N'komo* told me his demands. Here they are."

He cleared his throat noisily and spat.

"He asks that you come to Kouroula, walk seven times around his hut, from left to right, a rope around your neck, barking like a dog."

The lieutenant shook his head, smiled, and fell asleep.

He felt a burning, like a wasp's sting, opened his eyes, and scratched his forearm.

"Faganda!" he wailed.

He saw his brother picking his teeth with a green thorn.

"Yes, Siriman, what's wrong?"

The lieutenant stared at him, his face twisted in pain.

"Nothing."

And he went back to sleep.

After almost a month, the military doctor was caring for him in person, at the request of the governor.

"You understand," Bertin had said, "he has to accept his Legion of Honor. My rank and your promotion depend on it. And to accept the Legion of Honor, he has to live. You know that word of his arrest reached even the Minister of the Colonies?"

"And who nominated him for the Legion of Honor?"

"The governor, of course."

"But why?"

"A lieutenant of the French army converting to Islam and becoming a muezzin? We had to get him back."

"Astonishing!" the doctor groaned. "The wounds have healed, and the dog shows no symptoms of rabies. But then why this irregular pulse? This general weakening? And as if just to confuse things, these moments of delirium followed, especially at night, by periods of lucidity?"

"The lieutenant is under a spell," the nurse said.

"You make me laugh with your superstitions!" the doctor shouted. "Your job is to follow my orders, not to diagnose."

"Don't get mad, doctor. We Blacks avoid talking about it, but these spells exist."

Despite all the doctor's efforts, the patient's condition remained unchanged.

"Evacuate him to Darako," the commandant said, shrugging his shoulders.

"I'll fight; I'll beat this, Commandant!"

"Do as you like. The soldier conquered this country. And what heroism! Reread the story of the French penetration in West Africa. And especially in the savannah countries. The administrator has to maintain order, until our industrialists come to take all the riches that still slumber, ignored. The role of the colonial doctor has never been well-defined, alas . . ."

He stopped, lit a cigarette, furrowed his brow, and went out to the courtyard, the doctor following on his heels.

"After all, you can decorate someone posthumously. It's even more of an honor. Lieutenant Siriman Keita will be made a Knight of the Legion of Honor on Armistice Day. That's an order from the governor."

■   ■   ■

One morning, when the nurse was giving an injection, the doctor saw the patient turn his head and close his eyes. His breathing weakened. A sigh died in his throat. A tear clung to his eyelashes. The doctor took the lieutenant's hand, checked his pulse, and pressed an ear against his chest.

"It's over," he said to the nurse. "I don't understand. In your opinion, what did he die of?"

"Perhaps someone cast a spell on him?"

"Cast a spell? What does that even mean?"

"I don't know, doctor. I don't know any more."

"Well then, commit this to memory: the lieutenant died of viral hepatitis."

"Yes, doctor."

The village, alerted by Awa's shrieking, gathered at the square house. The imam washed his friend's body himself and wrapped it in a shroud.

Awa fell on her knees beside the body and, wracked with sobs, asked for her husband's forgiveness. The imam soberly recited the prayer for the dead without showing the least sign of emotion. And when he had finished, he moved to the middle of the circle, took off his burnous, and spread it over the lieutenant's body.

"I've decided that Siriman Keita will be buried in our mosque."

The funeral procession had just set off when a unit of guards appeared, rifles slung over their shoulders.

"The commandant has sent us to present military honors to the lieutenant, holder of the Croix de Guerre."

"Speak to the son of the deceased," the imam said.

"Several struggles for influence revolved around the lieutenant," Famakan said. "And it's to you that he belongs in the end."

The imam discreetly wiped away a tear.

"When a noble man dies, it's customary to honor his memory. That, the Whites did not invent."

"Then fire your rifles as much as you like!" Famakan shouted.

He took a rifle from one of the guards and cocked it.

"Seydou," he said, speaking to his younger brother, "push your finger there, on the trigger."

All those who owned rifles went to get them and joined the guards. They fired in unison all the way to the mosque, surrendering themselves to shouting and unbridled joy, as the odor of gunpowder drifted over Kouta.

Notes

1. *Boutou-ba*: a great insult to a woman's genitals.
2. *Kinkéliba*: leaves from which quinine can be extracted.
3. *Kotafla*: the two things that a man carries below.
4. *Sinsan*: tree of the savannah countries, the roots of which are added to various remedies.
5. Iblissa: Satan.
6. *Tara*: bamboo seat.
7. *Jahiliya*: pre-Muslim times, paganism.
8. N'komo: Mandinka secret society bound to agricultural rites; it demonstrates in a parade of dancers. [*N'komo* is used here in the singular to refer to the leader of the troupe of dancers. It is also used in the plural (non-italicized) to refer to the troupe of dancers and in the singular to refer to an animist witch doctor.—Trans.]
9. *N'komojeli*: griot of the N'komo.
10. Marka: an ethnic group associated with commerce, hence their exclusion from the secret societies of agricultural, sedentary groups.
11. *Bougounika*: a double-edged whip, produced in Bougouni, Mali, from which it derives its name.
12. *Bouda ha bou*: literally, "your behinds are full of shit."
13. *Ndeissane*: expresses pity but also admiration.
14. *Eh ndamansa*: Oh, God the Creator!
15. *Eh nba*: Oh, my mother!